## THE MAN WITHOUT A MIND

"Good morning."

Mitsuko nearly dropped her manifest. She spun around quickly to face the tall, sober-faced young man in the rumpled ship's coverall. A *Wild Goose* crew patch had been sewn to one breast pocket, brighter, newer than the fabric of the faded coverall.

"I'm Deke Hallorhan, your new pilot. You must be Mitsuko. Captain Callahan told me about you."

She had known him before he spoke, from Moses Callahan's memory—but Moses had not, *could not*, see the impossibility of Deacon Hallorhan.

Mitsuko couldn't hear him.

The words came through, clear and audible, but there was nothing else; no intruding stream of impressions and memories, no dark, roiling undervoice that might have warned her of his approach. There were only his words, disturbed air, ill-perceived and tenuous as some poorly learned and half-forgotten language, making no firm connection in her mind.

And an impossible telepathic silence.

### THE SHATTERED STARS
by Richard S. McEnroe

"Solid, entertaining space adventure, more readable than anything Clarke, Asimov, or Heinlein have turned out in the last twenty years."

—Charles Platt

# THE
# SHATTERED
# STARS

## RICHARD S. McENROE

**BANTAM BOOKS**
TORONTO · NEW YORK · LONDON · SYDNEY

THE SHATTERED STARS
A Bantam Book / January 1984

ISBN 0-553-23853-1

Published simultaneously in the United States and Canada

Bantam Books are published by Bantam Books, Inc. Its
trademark, consisting of the words "Bantam Books" and the
portrayal of a rooster, is Registered in U.S. Patent and Trademark Office and in other countries. Marca Registrada. Bantam
Books, Inc. 666 Fifth Avenue, New York, New York 10103.

# THE
# SHATTERED
# STARS

# THE
# SHATTERED
# STARS

# CHAPTER 1

They had taken Moses Callahan's ship and turned it into paper.

A man lived on his ship. He breathed her air, ate and drank from her stores. Her bulkheads solid around him kept the uncaring vacuum outside where it belonged and her driving engines bent the very curvature of space to take him wherever he wanted to go.

But then he had to land. . . .

Suddenly all that breathing and eating became a life-support replenishment invoice. Those protecting bulkheads hid structural support members that had to be inspected and recertified by a licensed and commensurately expensive naval surveyor. Engines became fuel costs and a ten-thousand-hour service charge. Then there were berth fees, entry fees, value-added tax on cargo transactions, customs "courtesy" fees, outright bribes to the longshoremen's union—and Moses Callahan wound up sitting in the deepest corner of the Hybreasil inport bar complex, wondering whether to have another beer or have his good uniform cleaned and pressed before heading outport to try to unearth a cargo Celtic Crescent or Western Galactic might have overlooked.

He ordered the beer, ignoring his cashplate's flickering scarlet reproach. The hovering waiter ejected his cashplate onto the table and floated off for his order, highlighted by the flickering glow of the alternate environment lounge—"A Touch of Elsewhere," the airlock announced—where shadowed figures moved through a chemical fog Moses would never have called air. The soft hiss of the waiter's jets was lost against the conversational susurrance of the

1

bar's other patrons, sharp young crew and officers off the corporate-line ships inport, who carefully did not see Moses in his shadowed corner and so were not compelled to the embarrassment of offering master's courtesies to a scabby independent. Moses welcomed their avoidance. He'd been that young once himself, and doubted they could tell him anything new and interesting about the condition.

He turned to watch the bartender, keying in orders for the waiters nursing docilely at the taps. The bartender was a fat old man with no hair to speak of and a good-natured expression, who wore a faded service tunic under his apron. Moses could see the brighter fabric where the globe and quadrangle of Fleet Arm had once been stitched: a veteran, too recently discharged to feel comfortable in civilian clothes yet. He'd probably hoarded his whole twenty years' pay just to set himself up with a starport bar, Moses imagined. Moses decided he liked the man. God knew, he envied him his security.

Maybe he should have stayed with the lines and gone the retirement route himself, he thought. Give him another ten or fifteen years and another thirty or forty pounds and he'd make a perfect uncle, telling outrageous lies to worshiping nephews while their mothers condemned him as a bad influence. But sitting behind his empty glass at his booth in the unfashionable corner of an anonymous starport bar, he was no such romantic figure. There was still enough sandy yellow mixed in with the gray hair to show that Moses Callahan was a man aging but not yet old. The thickening gut that broke the lines of his solid peasant's body and the loose skin on his square, thick-fingered hands added their own testimony. Moses Callahan was no longer a crisp young merchant officer on the way up, or yet a sedentary teller of tall tales for children, but a harried in-between—captain of a short-vector tramp with empty holds and empty pockets. He sat in his shadowed corner by the swirling mists of the nonterrestrial lounge, his only company the mindless peregrinating waiter, and only one man noticed him:

He was standing in the wide, arciform doorway of the windowless bar, momentarily blinded by the relative darkness after the daylight brightness of the street outside. He wore an expensive suit of the best quality, whose lines might have been cut to flatter the figure of a fifty-kilo male model but did nothing for his broad-shouldered, thick-waisted build. He had the muscular neck and slightly stooped posture of a man who had moved heavy objects for a living in the past, but the deep work-lines at the corners of his eyes and mouth had been softened by the flesh of more recent affluence. He looked around slowly, squinting against the gloom, until he saw Moses in his corner booth. Callahan discreetly palmed his flickering cashplate and pocketed it as the man approached.

"Good morning," the stranger said.

"'Day to you," Callahan said, in the soft, tired voice of a man who drank at ten-thirty in the morning.

"I'm looking for a Captain Callahan, off the *Wild Goose*."

"Happens you've found him, Mr.——?"

"Jakubowski." He slid into the empty seat facing Moses. "Axyll Jakubowski, Outward Bound Transfers and Storage."

"Have a seat," Moses said, sarcastically but with no special weight behind it.

"What are you drinking?"

"Richfield."

"Good choice." Jakubowski turned to the waiter gliding up to the table. "Two Richfields," he ordered, before Moses could correct him. The waiter deposited Callahan's own glass on the table and swept off to the bar. Jakubowski stared at the beer for a moment, then shrugged.

"That's the one thing wrong with Hybreasil," he said. "Best world in the region, but our own beer tastes like they poured the bauxite right into the vats."

"It's got a few other little flaws," Moses said.

Jakubowski frowned slightly. "Oh? I live here, friend. I'm *allowed* to bitch. What bothers a visitor like yourself?"

"Celtic Crescent, for one," Moses said. "Western Galactic, for another."

Jakubowski grinned. "Oh. Them. Don't forget Brendan Interstellar."

"What about them?"

"It was in the morning fax. Brendan's taking bids on a five-year compradore's license, with option to extend. I've got a bid in myself."

"Shit. This used to be a nice little port of call for a fellow going his own way."

Jakubowski shook his head. "Not anymore. Region's getting too big, too profitable. We're corporate-line territory now. Hell, you're only the third independent to call inport in the last six months, and I don't think either of the others would have got off the ground again if Mission House hadn't stepped in and found them cargoes."

"Now that's worth knowing," Moses said. "Maybe I should pay a call on Mission House myself."

"I doubt it would help. That was before *Boadicea* and *Western Comet* lifted out. Even Mission House can't find a cargo where there's none to be had. I think you're on your own, Captain, unless you want to put in for a Merchant Support Loan."

"No, thank you. I'm carrying enough paper already."

"Then you'll have to find a charter."

"So I will. What are you offering?"

"I'm looking to sign up a ship, if you're interested."

"If I'm interested. I owe fifteen thousand standards on this mudball, Mr. Jakubowski, whatever that comes to in the local play-money. Of course I'm interested."

"Do you know Avalon?"

"From the charts. I've never been there."

Jakubowski grimaced. "You haven't missed much. But I've got a consignment headed that way and it has to lift out in three days or I'm in breach of contract. I'll cover your port costs and ten thousand on top of that if you'll take it on."

"Port costs and twenty thousand."

"Where does a man about to have his ship attached get off bargaining?"

"You've been asking after me, then," Moses said.

"A man should know who he's dealing with."

"And so he should. But where does a man who needs to have a cargo off-planet in three days get off trying to starve an honest working man?"

"Fifteen thousand."

"Eighteen," Callahan said. "I'll need a decent stake for speculation when I hit the frontier again."

"Sixteen. What about your last run? You didn't come in here empty."

"Seventeen-five. I took a god-damned bath on my last run. The big lines have this sorry rock sewn up tight, remember?"

"Seventeen," Jakubowski said. "Maybe seventeen and a quarter, tops."

Now it was Callahan's turn to scowl back at him. "Now you're just being petty, man."

"All right, then. Seventeen-five, for a ship and crew to lift off no later than three days from today—what's the matter, Captain?"

"Nothing," Callahan said quickly. "But it'll be a bitch getting cleared to lift out in three days."

"Give my office your berth number and registry code. I'll run the processing and faxing through my organization." Jakubowski stood, producing a card and handing it to Callahan.

"Done," Callahan agreed. "You can embark your cargo in forty-eight hours."

Jakubowski grinned again. "Good." He stared down at Moses. "You surprised me, Captain. I thought for sure you'd want to know what you're carrying."

"Can I afford to make an issue of it?"

"I don't think so."

"Neither do I. Is it something I should consider making an issue of?"

"Not if you lift out on time."

"So that's how it is."

"Consider it as encouraging punctuality."

"I'll have to do that thing."

Jakubowski retreated back out into the daylight. Callahan reached for the extra beer and considered his improved fortunes. To go from insolvency to seventeen thousand standards flush—plus five hundred, of course—in five minutes was a good morning's work, even if he didn't really want to know how he was being asked to earn it. He'd handled cargoes on that basis before; like it or not, all independents had to, one time or another. And all he needed to handle this one was a stout crew, a tall ship, and a star to steer her by.

Two out of three, he thought. That was a start. . . .

# CHAPTER 2

Mitsuko Tamura welcomed the bulk of the machinery around her, and the illusion of privacy it afforded. Sweat beaded on her forehead beneath the heavy face shield and trickled down her temples as she slipped the tip of the soldering gun toward the broken feeder. She took comfort in the concentration such precise work demanded, directing the long tool with slender, supple fingers; it helped to push the mutterings further back in her awareness, to mute, briefly, the thousand tiny invasions of her every waking moment.

Otherwise she might have yielded to her constant urge simply to draw her legs up, slam the maintenance hatch shut behind her, and hide there until they all went away. . . .

She had a sudden flashing vision of the *Wild Goose* resting gracelessly in her concrete and girder berth, an unnatural nest for a mechanical evocation of bird-soul, coupled with a rush of affection she certainly didn't feel for the balky, aging hardware she did battle with daily. Moses was returning to his ship.

He was still halfway across the field. That wasn't unusual. This was his ship, imbued with enough of his presence to sensitize her to him to begin with. Beyond that, there was nothing subtle about Moses Callahan—he thought as clearly and loudly as some people spoke, announcing his passions and preoccupations of the moment with innocent vigor, and his sleep was a bright procession of vivid dreams that seldom lingered into wakefulness.

He was happy now, or at least happier than she'd felt him to be in the two weeks they'd spent on Hybreasil.

6

Mitsuko wondered how long that would last. He hadn't noticed the missing cable....

The *Wild Goose* was a blunt, gunmetal-gray wedge that seemed to crouch within her berth, as though waiting for a chance to spring clear of the tracery of catwalks and loading cranes surrounding her and leap back into the skies. But the tall intake vents for her atmospheric fans were slatted shut on her topsides, while the narrow ports that looked in on her underslung flight deck were empty and dark. She needed him, Moses thought, to put the breath back in her and restore the light of life and purpose to her eyes, and the prospect of a ship alive under his feet again was a glad thing.

The gladness broke against a quick spark of irritation when the passenger hatch ignored his key, remaining obstinately closed. Moses cursed and slid back the cover plate to the manual override.

"Spooky!"

The narrow passenger deck corridor was empty and dark, lit only by the sunlight admitted by the open airlock and the scattered glows of the emergency lanterns.

"Spooky!" Moses called again. "What the hell have you got the power off for?" Cursing, he turned and levered the airlock through its cycle again, cutting off the daylight. He stood blinking in the scarlet glow for a moment, then turned and started aft.

Mitsuko nearly landed on top of him as she dropped down through the drive-room ladderway. She didn't pause, but started forward toward the flight deck, with Callahan lumbering after her like a bear trying to follow a marten down its burrow.

"Dammit, Spooky, what the hell have you got the power down for?"

"I haven't got the power down, the port's got it down, Moses." She stopped at the bulkhead before them, to throw her full forty-five kilos' weight on the manual hatch lever. Callahan leaned past her and shoved it into place. The hatch slid open and she ducked in. "The port pulled our umbilical for nonpayment. When I went to cut in the on-board power, the converter blew out. I told you that was going to happen."

Callahan squeezed into the crowded flight deck. Grander starships, the handsome corporate-line giants that never saw the surface of a planet, never seared their gleaming hulls with the fires of reentry, could afford spacious bridges whose crews could lounge about with elbow room to waste while their captains strode about like officers and gentlemen, impressively upright and dignified. Not the *Goose*. There was the captain's station to port, with its terminal and repeater screens and the vector-shift board; the pilot's chair to starboard, and the engineer's tech pit squeezed in between structural members abaft the captain. A 'fresher stall and ration dispenser for short-handed watches—the only kind aboard the *Goose*—completed the crowded layout, just behind the pilot's station. There was barely headroom enough to seat Moses' one meter ninety without scraping his hat on the overhead, just legroom enough for a stiff stretch under the boards, and it had been the heart of Moses Callahan's universe for eleven years.

Mitsuko had climbed down into the tech pit, all but lost from sight behind consoles and crash padding. Callahan stooped and settled himself clumsily on the lip of the pilot's recess. The view through the narrow forward port-holes offered nothing save the uninspiring, heat-scored flank of an orbital barge.

The staccato sounds of a working keyboard rose from the tech pit and the panels around Callahan suddenly came to life, a swarm of green fireflies shot through with an alarming scatter of warning yellows. The familiar background noises of his ship surrounded him again, the susurrance of the ventilators, the buzzes and chimes of half a dozen telltales, the static-laced dialogues between Hybreasil port control and its traffic on the monitors. Mitsuko felt Moses relax behind her, a tenor threnody in the back of her mind settling down into the baritone.

"That's got it," she called. "At least until something else breaks."

"Nothing else is going to break," Moses said. Mitsuko braced herself against the sudden impulse to probe his certainty.

"Oh? Why not?"

"Because you're going to fix everything. Hell, I'll even let you buy some new spares, how does that sound?"

"Lovely. What am I supposed to buy them with?"

"Standards. Lots and lots of standards." Moses grinned. "I got us a charter, I did."

Mitsuko turned and looked up over the lip of the tech pit. For a moment she saw double, in spite of her control: Moses perched on the edge of the flight pit and a thick-necked man in a bar, loudly dressed and grinning.

"Come on," she said, "you weren't ashore nearly long enough to blackmail anybody."

"Did it take you all that time to come up with that? I'm serious. I got us a charter and we're lifting out in three days. All we need is a pilot."

Mitsuko's faith in the eternal verities was reaffirmed.

"All we need is a fifty kiloton liner with no payments due. All we need is a wealthy relative to die and leave us a million standards in gold. All we need is to have a break go our way for once. Guess what else we haven't got anymore, remember?"

"I know, I know, I know. So I'll get us one."

"You can't just buy a pilot at the chandlery, Moses. They're a little bit scarcer than second-hand converters."

"I'll get us a pilot. I'll go down to Mission House this afternoon. Hell, if it comes to it, I'll pilot her myself."

Mitsuko sighed. "When was the last time you had your ticket updated? For that matter, when was the last time you tried to pilot a ship by yourself?"

Moses frowned. "What was it, two years ago—no, three, three years, the time I took the paint off that revenue cutter—find a pilot," he chorused, half a word behind her. "Do you know what we need by way of stores?"

Mitsuko reached down and tapped at her keyboard. The fax-sheet printout by Moses' foot began to ticker out pages. Moses canceled the printout at the sixth; a seventh hung half-completed in the output slot.

"All right, all right, buy what you need. But don't get extravagant."

"I'm going to allow myself one luxury, at least," she said as she climbed out of the tech pit, dusting at her coveralls. "I'm ordering a new cleaning mech. This pit's a mess."

"Of course it's a mess. You never use it. You're always hiding off aft somewhere with your precious motors."

"I have to. If I wasn't there, who'd catch the little broken bits when they drop off?"

"Enough, enough. Go buy your fripperies."

"Current converters aren't fripperies, Captain, sir. But new gasket seals for the head in the master's cabin might be—and I'd hate to be extravagant."

"Dammit, you haven't fixed that *yet*?"

The cabin hatch slid shut behind her as Mitsuko flopped herself down on the narrow single berth. She hated her little sparring matches with Moses Callahan. They were necessary: she needed their glibness, their distancing effect, but they were dangerous as well. They could too easily go too far in either direction, into affection or anger, equally dangerous to her. And besides, Moses Callahan simply didn't deserve it. He was loud, but it was a clean loudness, simple and direct. Even the annoyance he had felt at finding the *Goose* blacked out was a straight-edged, short-lived thing, fading already. It wasn't in him to nurse an anger, to let it take root and fester in his mind and twist his thoughts. Even his undervoice, the dark, night-soil thoughts everybody had and too many people lived too much in, even that was almost a clean thing, compared to most.

And that was why she had to block him off, put up barriers of her own creation. She could not afford to fixate on his one mind alone, any more than she could open herself to the swirling thought-skeins of the city beyond the port and hope to survive. A person could drown as easily in six inches of water as in an ocean. . . .

. . . but now she had to work up her nerve to plunge headlong into that sea—she *had* to, in spite of the panic that threatened to overwhelm all her experience and training. She had to go out into that city, into the midst of all those thousands of loud, pushing, *thinking* people, because that was where she would find the parts she needed to make the *Wild Goose* a proper space-going craft again.

And she had to do that, because it was only up there, in the emptiness of lifeless, untenanted space, that she ever found anything resembling silence. . . .

# CHAPTER 3

Mission House was too humble a name for the power it signified.

The Confederate Mission for a major junction planet such as Hybreasil covered half a dozen city blocks on a side at the very center of the city. Other buildings might rise taller, gleam more brightly in the afternoon sun, aspire to greater architectural glory than the functional gray boxes that made up a Mission House—but in terms of the business conducted within, not one of them could match Mission House for prestige or influence.

Here was the Exchange, business nexus for twenty worlds. Men and women from the houses of the major compradores and a thousand smaller firms moved among the towering pale holograms with their flickering messages of profit and loss. Beyond and beneath the Exchange were the Warrens, where the strongest of those firms held their offices and economic competition became war, conducted by other means. Confederate Intelligence swept the Warrens periodically, not so much in hope of curtailing the more colorful business practices there as in the hope that those practices might have produced hardware new and interesting, worth issuing to its own operatives.

North of the commercial building, across the broad and verdant inner courtyard, was Government House, oldest building of the complex, a model in miniature for the structures that followed. It was not the capital of Hybreasil as such, although decisions were taken there that had as much effect on the colony as any law enacted in the PanDistrict Council. The various offworld embassies might keep elaborate offices in the taller, more prepossessing spires surrounding Mission House, or maintain luxurious lodges in the outlying agrarian districts, but they conducted their real business in Mission House, where the Confederacy's Agent oversaw the maneuvering between worlds. The Council could pass its legislation, and the embassies could strike their bargains, but it was the Agent who controlled the Regional Fleet Arm units insystem and ensured that the interest of the Confederacy was felt in the affairs of its wards. And it was to the ground floor of Government House that Moses Callahan came, to the offices of the Bureau of Shipping and Mariner's Hall: two small, aged rooms, all the space deemed necessary to attend to the shoreside end of the thread that linked the worlds.

The holograms in Mariner's Hall parted as he walked through them, looking for the roster of available pilots. Deck crew, engineers, stewards . . . the listings were thin, shot through with large gaps where blocks of names had been stricken off. The arrival of the major lines was having its effect. The pool of available independent spacers was draining rapidly as trained men and women anticipated the coming dearth of independent berths and lifted out in the first available spaces. The independents were fleeing Hybreasil. Sometime in the next year or so they would begin to cluster again, on some less prominent world farther out, and the cycle of development and supplantation would recommence, closer to the expanding frontier.

The pilot's block was empty—almost.

There was one name, far down the translucent blue block, on a line with Moses' knee. He knelt and stared unhappily at the line of pale script. *Deacon James Hallorhan*—the name meant nothing to Moses, conjured up no face out of the circle of spacers Callahan had met in his twenty-nine years of faring. But he was there on the board, with a valid certification code and a current registration number—and according to the date displayed he had been sitting inport for the last three months, in subsidized Mission lodgings. Moses didn't have to look up at the master board to check his numbers—there had been one independent and three corporate ships through Hybreasil in those three months, and none of them had seen fit to sign this pilot. That just didn't happen; everybody needed pilots. They jumped from independent to independent the way fleas jumped from dog to dog, and the bigger corporate-line ships would always sign on a licensed pilot, if only for deep manpower reserve. The turnover was such that a good pilot could write his own ticket and a merely competent one was still assured of a berth on some ship or other. Only the dregs, the incompetents, the druggies, the heavy drinkers, or the bizarros sat grounded for any length of time, particularly on a corporation-served world. Moses wondered what was wrong with this Deacon James Hallorhan—and then he wondered why he bothered to wonder. He was in no position to be fussy.

He stood and brushed through the holograms to the waiting clerk.

"I'm Moses Callahan, captain, of the *Wild Goose*, registered on Og Eirrin. I'd like to meet with Ship's Pilot Deacon Hallorhan, if he's available, with a view toward his signing articles."

"Certainly, Captain," the clerk said. "I'll have him paged, if you'd care to wait here."

"No, that's all right," Moses said. "Have him meet me in the lounge, please."

"Of course, sir. Anything to get him off our hands."

"Oh, wonderful."

"Captain Callahan?"

He was a young man, tall and slightly stooped, with a shock of unruly black hair escaping from under the brim of his crumpled Fleet Issue yard cap. His tunic hung loosely on wide, bony shoulders, its empty folds suggesting that there might once have been more to Deacon Hallorhan than now met the eye.

He looked as though he hadn't slept a day in his life.

"Deacon Hallorhan?" Callahan asked.

"Deke," he said, shrugging. "Or Deacon. Whatever. You're Captain Callahan?"

"The same. Take a seat." Callahan signaled for the waiter. "What'll you have?"

"Richfield, as long as you're buying."

"You've got expensive tastes for someone who's been grounded for three months."

"There isn't much to spend back pay on in a House flat."

"No."

"Besides, try drinking the local stuff and you won't have any taste at all. I think they put the cans inside the beer down here."

Moses chuckled. "You're the second person who's told me that today."

"So consider yourself warned."

"Thanks." Moses' grin faded. "To business, then. I'm after needing a pilot, Deacon, and Mariner's Hall shows you as the only one available."

"Uh-huh. For the last three months. And that worries you."

"Just so."

Hallorhan reached into his tunic. "I guess you'll want to see my book." He pulled out a slim bound folio, his spacer's ticket—identification, passport, and job history all in one. No honest spacer ever willingly parted with it, or hesitated to show it to a prospective employer.

It told Moses nothing he wanted to hear.

Deacon James Hallorhan, thirty-four, one meter ninety-one centimeters tall, weight ninety-eight kilograms (that had certainly changed), hair black, eyes blue. Served with the Confederate Fleet Arm, Mishima Flotilla, honorably discharged with a small pension, medical reasons, mustered out with the adjusted rank of lieutenant—

Moses frowned at the book. If it was an honorable discharge, why the pension? Why not a medical discharge? Why the adjusted rank upon mustering out? Moses had never heard of a rank adjusted in the individual's favor. . . .

—attended the Merchant Academy of Nova Genoa on veteran's benefits, picked up his pilot's ticket there. Nova Genoa had a fine academy. A ticket from NGMA was a plus for any spacer. But—

"You picked up your ticket after your discharge, Deacon?"

"That's right."

"What was your occupation with Fleet?"

"Marine Infantry. The Two-twenty-third."

"From Marine Infantry to pilot?"

"It's easier on the feet. And I figured the hours would be better."

"Ah."

Moses touched the page tab and the infinitely divisible hologram block flickered to display Hallorhan's employment history: The *Amerigo* from Nova Genoa to Hansen System, eighteen months aboard. The *Datter Mi* from Wolkenheim to the Arcadian Worlds, nine months aboard. The *Industrious* from Peng's Paradise to the West Star system and Hybreasil.

And not one ship's master had a negative word to say about Deacon Hallorhan. All his releases were on good terms, his profit shares and salary well within the expected range for a competent pilot. And the reference comments were the same for each ship. "Services Most Acceptable." "Entirely Competent." "Performance Entirely Adequate." Yet for all that acceptability, competence, and adequacy, each ship had let him leave—and that just didn't ring true.

Shipmasters simply didn't let go of capable pilots without a fight; they were too valuable. Captains might handle a ship's profits and losses, and handle the actual FTL transitions themselves; engineers might keep a ship running; stewards might keep a ship's passengers fat and happy. But pilots got the ships on and off the ground in one piece. If a pilot could find the ground right side up, captains would raise their salaries, fatten their shares, even alter their routes if the pilot was good enough. Yet *Industrious*, *Datter Mi*, and *Amerigo* hadn't done that. "You're a perfectly good pilot," they had said to Deacon Hallorhan, "good-bye."

It was wrong. Moses found himself suddenly, intensely suspicious of the bland, approving tone of those brief recommendations. A spacer's ticket was a permanent record. Faced with that permanence, a great many masters had let go marginal crew in the past with an attitude of saying nothing at all if they couldn't say anything nice. Moses had fattened more than one ticket in just that manner himself in his day.

"I'm afraid I'm going to commit a breach of spacer's etiquette," Moses said. "Why did you leave *Industrious*?"

Hallorhan smiled, without much enthusiasm. "I walked out, Captain, I wasn't thrown out. Do the details matter?"

"Maybe they do."

Hallorhan nodded, once. "You're right. That is a breach of etiquette, Captain."

"I know it," Callahan said, "and I wouldn't ask, usually. But you've got an uncommon book here, Deacon. You go from playing soldier to piloting starships. You've got discharge terms I've never heard of. And you've got three captains here that each say you're a perfectly good pilot, and each one of them let you go. Now, what kind of captain lets a perfectly good pilot go?"

"Those three did. Maybe you should ask them that."

"And wouldn't it be nice if I could?" Moses said. "But I can't. So I'm asking you."

Hallorhan stood. "I think this was a mistake. Thanks for the beer."

"Hold it there," Callahan said. "I am getting very tired of everybody I meet on this slag heap carrying on as if they haven't a care in the world when they're in as deep a hole as I am. Now if I don't take you on, Deacon, chances are very, very good that there won't be another independent through here for another six months. This planet's going corporate-line, and the smart folk are getting out of the way. On top of that, Mission House isn't going to be too happy if you keep hanging around here. They don't like people setting up housekeeping in House lodgings for life, and if you try to hang on here much longer, they're just liable to line you up a charity berth on the next scow as comes inport, and see that you get on it. They can do that, you know."

"Yeah," Hallorhan said glumly. "I know they can."

"Now, I need a pilot, and you're the only pilot available, but I'll be damned if I'll put you under articles before I'm certain you're no hazard to my ship. So if you don't want to answer my question, you go ahead and walk. But if you want a berth on my ship, you will by God talk to me."

Moses watched as Hallorhan stared past him, coming to a decision.

"They'd gone as far as they were going," he said. "They were going to start back toward Mishima Sector, complete their circuits. I've *been* there, Captain. All I want from Mishima Sector is away."

"Old war stories, Lieutenant?"

"Something like that," Hallorhan said.

"Well, that's nothing I have to know about. So you'll only work the outbound leg? You'll cut a hell of a piece off your share that way."

"The money doesn't matter. The going does."

"All right." Callahan put out his hand. "You're under articles, if you want to be."

"I want. What are you flying?"

"The *Wild Goose*, Dock Nine. She's a Wander Bird short-vector tramp, you can't miss her."

"A Wander Bird? That's a pretty well-established class."

"Which is your polite way of saying she's a prehistoric tub."

"Hell, no. I've seen—and flown—older, Captain."

"But not much," Callahan said.

"Well, no. . . ."

"I thought not. She's an antique, all right. But she's *my* antique."

"Good enough. Where're we bound?"

"Avalon."

"Avalon?" Hallorhan frowned. "Jakubowski's deal?"

"How'd you know about that?"

"I've been sitting here for three months, Captain. What else did I have to do but keep my ears open?"

"And what have those ears heard?"

"Axyll Jakubowski's been pushing a midnight deal at every independent that's come inport for the last year, from what I heard. Nobody's taken him on before. He seems to be a little too shy about specifics for anyone to trust him—or take him seriously, maybe."

"Probably no one was broke enough before. I wish more and more I knew what he was trying to ship."

"*Western Ranger*'s shuttles are down and loading. Maybe he's approached them first," Hallorhan said.

Moses shook his head. "He wouldn't take a midnight deal to a corporate ship. They wouldn't risk their charters for the kind of money an Axyll Jakubowski could be worth."

"No, probably not." Hallorhan paused. "Listen, do you really want to know what he's shipping?"

"Of course."

"I think I could find out."

"How?"

Hallorhan smiled his unenthusiastic smile again. "Don't ask and no one will blame you for not telling. Let me check a few places I know."

"Everybody's got secrets," Moses complained. "All right.

But don't mention the ship while you're about it. And be aboard tomorrow afternoon."

"Aye, aye, sir." His grip, when he reached over the table and took Moses' outstretched hand, was as strong as Moses' own.

*He leaped clear of the drop boat as it burned around him, landing pack flaring. Six meters above the ground he cut the pack free and dropped, taking the shock of the landing in his armored legs and going with it into a forward tuck-and-roll meant to throw off any targeting gunners. But the drop boat was still drawing the Mishimans' defensive fire; it slewed away clumsily in a flare of jets and steaming ablative as laser fire and missiles broke it open and dropped it flaming to the pocked tarmac of the port. There was no going home now, not unless they won time enough to carve out and hold a secure pickup zone, but Hallorhan wasn't thinking about retreat. Specials weren't supposed to. The platoon was moving out, thirty-six heavy-metal thunder-rapers psyched on gung-ho speeches, firepower, and high-mike bouncers, and he was supposed to be moving out with them. That was all he had to worry about.*

*He leaped, current flowing from his enerpacs through the striated "muscle" tissues of his symbioplast armor. The pseudoliving plastic flexed to match the input action of thighs and calves and arching back; alloyed exoskeletal hinges supported organic joints that would have been torn in half under such strains. He landed in the cover of the tail vanes of a wrecked cutter. He looked around, selected a target, and jumped again.*

*The jump carried him through the line of fire of one of the whirling two-barrel lasers. Its pulses stabbed harmlessly past him with far more power than they needed to kill one man. The weapon was still firing in its ship-killing mode; it took too long to recycle between the heavy pulses for the laser to lay out an effective antipersonnel pattern.*

*He came down in the gunpit, and the Krupp pulser in his hand speared the man before him with a lance of solid light. His left-hand plasma gauntlet vomited a streamer of incandescent energy and a second man fell back, screaming, wreathed in blue flame, to scatter the rest of the guntechs as he was consumed. The uncontrolled laser traversed blindly, its unguided fire stabbing away into the dawn sky over the port. Hallorhan twisted as he jumped again, bringing the Krupp to bear on the two-barrel as he cleared the lip of the gunpit. He fired.*

*The detonation of the weapon's enerpac was directed upward by the walls of the gunpit even as they vanished, but the fractional concussion that did reach him was still enough to tumble him like a leaf. He overrode his stabilizers and took the fall sloppily, rolling underneath the point where three sparks of actinic light converged, fire that would have cut him apart had he landed upright. Then he was on his feet and running forward, feeling good, in control, as he raced for the burning buildings where the Mishiman infantry was trying to rally. He wouldn't let them, he decided, the training and the augmented speeches and the little sky-blue pills working perfectly.*

*He could see figures moving through the smoke and flames, the hulking, armored shapes of his teammates moving faster than anything so massive had any right to, advancing out of the port and into the city beyond. Fire began to seek them out, not organized yet but heavy. Bar-straight laser bolts and fluid bursts of glaring blue plasma cut across one another between the paler flames of the burning buildings. Luminous arrowheads appeared on the inside of Hallorhan's visor, picking out Mishiman gunners. He cut in autofire and watched with detached interest as his gun arm swung up and the Krupp began pumping light with microcircuited precision into its designated targets. The arrowheads began to wink out, almost as fast as new ones appeared, new opponents springing up as the old ones were eliminated.*

*Sudden movement to his left brought him swinging around—but not in time to lase the Mishiman who threw himself into Hallorhan's chest. The armor's tactile sensors conveyed the rasp of the gun muzzle along his ribs perfectly. Hallorhan released the Krupp to snap back into its holster and drove his fist with all the amplified strength of his armored arm behind it into the Mishiman's chest. The Mishiman was wearing standard infantry cladding, which would block most shrapnel and sliver fire and even turn a hand laser for a moment. He might as well have been wearing silk. Hallorhan felt the man's sternum collapse under his punch. He ignored the Mishiman as he was thrown back against the burning wall broken and dying. The Krupp snapped back out into his hand at his willed command and he turned away, back to the battle.*

*He didn't need the arrowheads strobing against his faceplate to tell him the Mishimans were still out there. Lasers and plasma charges stabbed wildly in all directions; his audio pickups whistled constantly with the passage of high-velocity rifle slivers. He kept moving forward—as if the pills would have let him stand still—dodging constantly, untouched save for the burst of two-by-fifty slivers that shattered against his thigh with the sting of a dozen wire whips. The Krupp was tracking and firing continuously, seeking out and piercing target after target, one faceless, visored Mishiman mannequin after another. They died in the distance, their passing marked only by the disappearance of a glowing arrowhead, or they died right in front of him, burnt or cut through or broken but always ciphers, for he never saw anything in their visors save the distorted reflection of his armored form, as anonymous as any of them, as he killed them.*

*He leaped, and the ground shook with more than the impact of his landing as the first artillery salvo dropped among the advancing Specials. His audio pickups damped out at once, and for a moment all he could hear was the jubilant war cries of the platoon turned to startled shouts across the tac channels. There was no panic, no alarm— they had all been fed their sky-blue Fleet Issue cure for that—and there were no cries of pain, either. Anything that could pierce Special armor would knock out transceiver circuits as quickly as it killed the man or woman wearing it.*

*The ground lurched again, and the burning building to his right gave up and crumbled in upon itself, sending a wave of fiery rubble rushing out into the street as flames billowed up into the sky. Hallorhan jumped to avoid the entangling wreckage, and his leap sent him headlong through the shattered window before him, into fire.*

*The burning room licked at his armor with incandescent tongues, even as his carapace mirrored over to repel its heat, even as the first suffusing warmth seeped through to*

*warn of its impending failure. Hallorhan lunged forward,
through a door that slowed his passing not at all in its
destruction, into the corridor beyond.*

*Everything was flame: the walls burned, the ceiling
swirled with fire, the floor beneath his feet smoked and
buckled under his weight. He ran, ponderous in the
confined space of the corridor, unable to leap and use the
suit to its fullest advantage.*

*The heat built; sweat trickled down his face faster than
the armor's fans could dry it; a warning display spoke of
the increasing pressure in the bottles as the gasses of his
life-support system expanded and strained against con-
straining metal.*

*The corridor seemed endless. The doors at its far end
rippled with false distance, obscured by fire and the
steady rain of falling detritus. Hallorhan rushed toward
them, running the gauntlet of fiery debris and the waving,
entrapping ornamental panels sprung from the walls by
the intense heat. The flimsy panels he struck aside; the
flames he ignored, for want of any power over them.*

*The doors ruptured outward in a shower of alloy and
glass and he was through them, into the open again—and
facing the mass of Mishiman infantry running down the
street, weapons at the ready.*

*It never occurred to Hallorhan, just as it had never
occurred to the men who had trained him, and psyched
him, and fed him his baby-blue courage, to turn aside, to
avoid a direct confrontation with such a concentrated
force. He had not been shaped with a conventional soldier's capacity for retreat in mind; that wasn't a Special's
function—quite exclusively the opposite. He went forward.*

*The Mishimans scattered, bringing their weapons up.
The inside of Hallorhan's visor was a cross-hatched maze
of arrowheads and indicators telling him what he already
knew as he closed with the enemy, his Krupp swinging into
line.*

*A blurred shape rushed past Hallorhan from behind. He
nearly burned it through before he recognized the Special
armor. The Special's cry shrilled in Hallorhan's pickups, as
shrill and chillingly anachronistic as the Mishimans' own
spirit-shouts. Give a madman the destructive power of a*

*raging demigod and he might make such a noise, in celebration of license—*

*—A madman did, Hallorhan realized, and he reveled in the liberty the realization granted him. He added his own fire to his companion's, his own shout burst from his throat—*

*A Mishiman pointed the bulky tube of a man-portable missile at the Special ahead of Hallorhan, and fired even as he died. Powerful enough to cripple an armored gunship, the missile spent its full strength against the body of a single man.*

*The blast staggered Hallorhan. Only his stabilizers held him upright as he stumbled through the Mishimans, firing blindly with plasma and laser, his awareness locked on the trailing lengths of charred viscera draped over his arms and chest—*

—The small room was dark and quiet, quieter certainly than his sleep. Hallorhan sat bolt upright in the spartan bed he called his own for as long as Mariner's Hall tolerated his presence. Exhaling shakily, heavily—it might almost have been a sob if he could have admitted he had anything to cry about—he reached over and keyed in the room lights, defining the cramped confines of his cubicle, preferring its bland pastel walls to the incarnadine garishness of his memory. The lifter grids of the bed canted gently and slid him to his feet facing the inset mirror and the narrow shelf, the sunken drawers. He studied his reflection blearily. Seventy-three kilos left out of ninety-eight, any tan long gone but the wrinkles burned in by marches under a dozen suns still indelibly etched, hair thinning prematurely from the constant erosion of tight helmet padding, no property to his name that didn't fit easily into the stuffed two crewpacs, packed the drawers unemptied before him: not a whole hell of a lot to show after a third of a man's alotted five score—but screw that, he thought, he was still there to add it up; he'd settle for that. He'd have to.

The shelf in front of him was bare except for the two small pill bottles: the half-empty phial of bouncers that kept him awake, kept him in the present, and the prescription sleepers he kept out of obedient habit, although their service was the last thing he wanted. Even his sleep failed him now.

He tapped out two more bouncers and washed them down with lukewarm water from the cubicle tap. Transients didn't warrant anything more elaborate in the line of toilet facilities, not on the eyes of Mariner's Hall. He debated the trip down the hall to the floor's common 'fresher and decided against it. For what he had to do a good feeling of three-aye-em griminess would just about get him in the mood.

He opened the topmost drawer and pulled a reasonably unwrinkled ship's coverall from the crewpac. The handle of the middle drawer brushed coldly against his bare knee and he paused for a moment, remembering the second crewpac, cataloguing its contents and desiring them too dearly. He diverted himself by slamming the top drawer shut, noticing that the strip of artiflesh over the terminals in his right wrist had come adrift. He brushed it back into place and the terminals were gone again, wiped from sight even if he could never wipe them away. . . .

Put enough people in one place, and there's no one there.

Take a virgin canvas, paint, a brush. The first strokes are unique, individual, as recognizable for themselves as for the pattern they compose. Paint further, and the strokes begin to lose their identity; the effect of their aggregate begins to predominate. Paint further, and the strokes become invisible; the pattern itself may be lost in their overwhelming profusion. A street is no different.

The great signs of woven light outshouted each other into incomprehensibility. Scarlet and pale blue, electric orange and alamogordium green, they advertised their addresses, proclaimed their products, and banished night from the city, leaving only darkness. No natural light could compete with their glare; a man might live out his life under their mercenary illumination and never see the stars that exported the myriad products they hawked.

Under such lights, even the people thronging the crowded streets were reduced. Color of dress and hair and skin was washed away and replaced by the garish glow of salesmanship; facial features were reduced to shifting pools of light and shadow; textures of fabric and skin were flattened into grainy plasticity.

Hallorhan moved anonymously through the jostling crowds, sidestepping the hucksters, edging around the bowed-shouldered pedestrians who slowed abruptly in their courses as though shot through the soul by some karmic sniper, the life-strength they needed to breast the onrushing torrent of light and sound leaching away uselessly into the frantic kinetic vacuum of the street. There was nothing to distinguish him from any of them: over his ship's coverall he wore a light, unlined liberty jac with the NGMA crest woven across its back in the florid Gothic script they favored there. Ship's patches from *Amerigo*, *Datter Mi*, and *Industrious* adorned its shoulders and left breast, a unit crest from the Two Hundred and Twenty-third Marine Infantry—Victory From On High—the right. His crumpled Fleet Issue yard cap rode on his head, pushed back. He looked like every other grounded spacer looking for liberty outport, like every city-born adolescent who bought his adventures from the surplus clothing outlets. But the lights could not mark him; they could put no shadows under his eyes darker than those the bouncers and his dreams put there naturally. The crowd was something apart from him, distant; he passed among them with no more real contact than he felt whenever he walked through one of the holographic meat-show signs that hovered in the air above the sidewalks. In that, he was the exact opposite of the urban street-lunatics stumbling through the streets and hunched over in the doorways, mumbling their every random thought and impression back into the streets that inspired them, for whom the difference between out in the world and inside their heads had long ceased to be any difference at all. That he was, perhaps, no more sane than any of them was something he knew he accepted far more docilely than he should have.

The noise didn't bother him, not the traffic nor the advertisements of the passersby nor the madmen staggering shrieking out from between artistically spread thighs; not the meat-show barkers nor the peddlers nor the spastic ululations of distant sirens. He remembered killing a city. Traffic honking in protest of a double-floated cab was by comparison no distraction.

He ignored the dancing lights of the ads as easily, even the ad for the fully automatic tourist-special holiday recorder that towered hundreds of feet into the air above the colorful city life the tourists were meant to record, transfixing the milling crowds in its optic element in an insane infinite loop of mutual snapshooting. Hallorhan's needs for the good life reduced quite simply to avoiding his dreams and fleeing their inspiration. And he sure as hell didn't need a fully automatic tourist-special holiday recorder to lock in *his* memories.

The sales pitches couldn't touch him. The mental keys they were supposed to punch, the emotional buttons they were meant to push were out of their reach, conditioned and suppressed for convenience and efficiency, later blocked away completely, out of fear. Not his convenience, not his efficiency, not his fear, but it was too late for Hallorhan to worry about that now. Besides, the parts of himself that used to worry about such things were some of the bits that had been buried most deeply. . . .

He turned the corner, off the main drag, into other, darker streets. Now there were no ads, no tourists for them to pitch to, no peddlers or barkers or whores to prey on the tourists, all prudently gathered out on the main drag where the guidebooks said they were safe from such things. The madmen here lacked the enthusiasm or the strength to mutter and shriek entertainingly; their fading awarenesses extended no farther than the stoops of their doorways. The streets were still, funereal: the light from the main drag around the corner lit the sky above the rooftops like the nimbus of a fire that had swept through this neighborhood long since, leaving nothing but the shells of buildings and last week's litter. Hallorhan walked for several blocks under the intermittent glow of the scattered working streetlights. He stayed well out in the street, far from the doorless mouths of the derelict buildings.

Hallorhan turned another corner, and the neighborhood changed again. Now he walked along a street of warehouses, their loading ramps shut, their streetfronts lit by harsh security floodlamps. Here and there the more prestigious storage firms could afford the luxury of a guard shack, picked out by the pale blue glow of their security monitors.

Outward Bound Transfers and Storage was one of these. The small prefabricated guard hut stood out by the street, the mouth of the hauler's-width driveway running the length of the building. From his vantage point across the street, Hallorhan could see the bored guard at his desk and the video pickup high on one wall, panning back and forth. That was good; in fact, it was the best arrangement he could hope for. When a monitor system was intended for serious surveillance, its pickups were seldom visible and their observer never was. When the pickups were out in the open, when the man running them was in plain sight, it meant that the system was meant to deter by its very obviousness, not its unseen, efficiency. More, it was a safe bet that the one guard in his shack was the only guard on duty—that was the sort of false economy such a slap-dash arrangement encouraged.

Hallorhan moved on up the block out of sight of the guard shack before he crossed and came back along the guard's blind side. He leaned carefully around the corner and looked in through the streetside window. The monitors were flickering away pointlessly, the watchman's attention focused on the pornicart's erotic display on the table before him. Every now and then, when a shoulder or knee obscured the best view, the guard would glance up at the monitors, but there was no doubting where his full concentration lay.

Ducking, Hallorhan slipped past the booth, then stood and moved toward the sliding doors at the end of the driveway. He kept to the wall the first pickup was mounted on, moving steadily but slowly. He could see the gleam of a second imaging element at the far end of the driveway, looking down its entire length—but he would be virtually invisible at the wide angle it would be set for. As long as he avoided any sudden, extreme motion, he would pass unnoticed. The steady panning of the pickup would mask his cautious advance.

Hallorhan sidled under the first camera, out of its line of vision. The employees' entrance to the warehouse was just meters away, across the driveway. He waited until the pickup at the end of the driveway had panned all the way across to the wall where he stood, and then crossed, matching his pace to the movement of the pickup.

In the doorway, he was safe. The shadow of the sill was the best cover in the driveway. He looked back to the guard shack; the watchman hadn't stirred.

Hallorhan studied the door. The lock slot seemed conventional enough, and there was no sign of any external alarm system.

Hallorhan took the key blank from his pocket. It was a freshly bought copy, unprogrammed as yet; the short strands of wire and the male jacks soldered on were his own additions. He peeled back the strip of artiflesh over the terminals and fitted the jacks into the sockets on his wrist, the sockets that once linked him to the tactile, motor, and autofire circuits of a suit of Special armor, but that now would serve his own purposes.

The lock signals were gibberish, tiny spider's footsteps across the back of his skull, unlike the remembered clarity and order of sensor and weapon inputs. Hallorhan reached back into his mind, just like in the drills, trapping the signals and nailing them down, one by one, locking them into a coherent sequence. The signals evaded him, laid deceitful little traps for him: pattern upon pattern seemed to make perfect sense but left the machinery of the lock inert and unresponsive. But Hallorhan was not limited by the need to physically generate new sequences. As fast as he could think of them, faster than he could even become aware of them, the Special circuitry fed new combinations into the lock. He was scarcely even conscious of the process itself; he sought nothing so much as to generate a proper *feeling* of order in the lock—and when that feeling came upon him, the lock undid itself with a sharp metallic report.

He took his last risk when he opened the door and slipped into the warehouse itself. There had to be at least one internal pickup, and the sudden flash of light from the opening door was more likely to catch the guard's eye than anything else Hallorhan had done so far. He slipped through and shut the door quickly, and waited in the semidarkness of the warehouse for any response from outside. Nothing. He began his search.

He was looking for a fairly substantial parcel. Had Jakubowski's midnight cargo been anything easily portable, he would simply have shipped it concealed in a hireling's luggage. If he was approaching captains about carrying it openly, it had to be something too big to hide.

It wasn't hard. After *Boadicea* and *Western Comet*, with *Western Ranger* down and loading, there probably wasn't a crowded warehouse in the city. This one was all but empty. There were a scant half-dozen crated cargoes left resting on their pallets, no more.

The first three were nothing. Domestic liquors, only as marketable as they were exotic—in this case, not very; handicrafts from the outlying agrarian districts, not quite vigorous enough to be primitive, not quite sophisticated enough to qualify as modern art; clothing of deliberately quaint local homespun. Hallorhan wasn't surprised that these hadn't appealed to the corporate ships. They were the sort of thing a captain might take on speculation, strictly for their curiosity value, and corporate-line captains had no need to speculate.

The fourth crate was smaller than the others, but far more sturdy. *Industrial electronics*, the stenciling read, *Heavy*. The lid was fastened strongly, actually screwed down tight rather than being simply banded or latched shut. Hallorhan appropriated a welded sculpture from the handicrafts shipment and managed, with a protruding edge of twisted steel, to defeat the stubborn fastenings. He peered into the shadowed recesses of the crate, squinting at the lettering stenciled on slate-gray metal.

"Oh, shit."

"A Bethe trigger," Hallorhan said. "That lunatic's got himself a Bethe trigger, Captain, and he's suckered you into running it for him."

"Calm down," Moses said. The unfolded desk and chair left little room in the compact master's cabin for Hallorhan's nervous pacing. "Nobody's conned me into anything until I land on Avalon, and maybe not even then. Now, what the hell is a Bethe trigger? A weapon, I take it. Some kind of bomb, isn't it?"

"Not exactly." Hallorhan checked his pacing and sat down heavily on the edge of Moses' bunk. "A Bethe trigger *makes* bombs."

"Does it, now? Out of what?"

"Anything you like," Hallorhan said. "Dirt, rock, water,

air, trees, you, me, anything. You know the Bethe Solar Phoenix?"

"I'm not entirely unschooled."

"Yeah, well, a Bethe trigger initiates a Solar Phoenix reaction, only it isn't limited to stellar matter under stellar conditions."

"Good God."

"Uh-huh. Calibrate it for any element you want—nitrogen, carbon, silicon, anything—and for as long as the Bethe catalyst lasts you get a little baby star, Captain, anyplace you like. Cute, huh?"

"Adorable. A star in the middle of a city."

"Or a continent. Or a planet. Set one for hydrogen and drop it in an ocean, that'll give you a real show."

"Dear sweet Christ. How big do these things get?"

"Depends on the catalytic charge, and how much you've got of whatever element you calibrated for."

"How big is this one?"

Hallorhan shrugged. "I told you, it depends. But I'll tell you this much—Fleet Arm doesn't *use* little bombs, and Bethe triggers are exclusively Fleet Issue. Or they used to be." He shook his head. "Jakubowski's got a gadget out there that can turn this city and everyone in it into so much sunshine . . . and you're loading it on board tomorrow."

"The hell I am," Moses said.

"The hell you're not, Captain."

"Oh?"

"Oh." Hallorhan was back on his feet, pacing his tight circle again. "Where do you think somebody like Jakubowski got hold of a Bethe trigger?"

"I'm sure he asked for it nicely."

"He got it from Fleet, or from someone in Fleet. No place else. Bethe triggers aren't common black-market stock. They're built in Fleet arsenals, they're shipped in Fleet carriers, deployed in Fleet support centers, and they stay there unless directly authorized by the Sector Agent General himself. They don't even issue them to the border squadrons without SAG approval."

"What are you telling me, now?" Moses asked.

"I'm telling you that Jakubowski's the least of your worries. It's whoever gave him the trigger that scares me."

"And what should I do about that?"

Hallorhan sagged back into a corner of the cabin, hands jammed into his pockets, staring at the bare metal deck. "I don't think there's a hell of a lot you can do, Captain. You don't know who gave Jakubowski the trigger, or why. You do know that they're pretty well connected, probably with somebody in Fleet itself. Maybe they even *are* Fleet."

"They probably are," Moses said. "These triggers don't sound like the sort of thing that falls off the back of a hauler."

"They're not."

"And Jakubowski's been pushing this deal for a year now?"

"That's the word."

"Then if I went to the authorities and reported it—"

"Whoever Jakubowski's friend is would hear about it. You might even be talking to him." Moses looked at him, puzzled. "Fleet doesn't play revenuer as a rule, Captain, but they do like to keep track of what's changing hands around them."

"I didn't know that."

"I guess you've never run guns before. Hell, I didn't know it either, until my outfit pulled boarding duty with the interdiction cutters off Leibensraum. Fleet likes to know what people are going to be shooting at them with."

"So Jakubowski's friend has to be Fleet, doesn't he?"

"I guess. He couldn't have had the trigger all this time—but he did have to be able to get his hands on one the minute he needed it. There's no way he could guarantee that without some very high level help."

"And they'd probably help him keep his little secret, too, wouldn't they?"

"Fatally."

"Shit."

"Succinct, but not very helpful."

"Nor shall I be," Moses said. "Maybe I can't risk telling anybody about this mess, but I sure as hell don't have to be part of it. Jakubowski can take his toy to some other ship. I'm out."

"No, you're not."

"You keep saying that."

"'Cause I'm right. I am getting very tired of everybody I meet on this slag heap carrying on as if they hadn't a care

in the world when they're in as deep a hole as I am,'
remember? You gonna pull this old girl out of that hole
without Jakubowski's money?"

"Damn you," Moses said. Hallorhan didn't react. "You
think I don't have some kind of principles? You think I put
keeping my ship above getting involved in a mess like
this?"

"Of course you do."

"Goddamned right. But now that I *am* involved, I'll just
have to see it through. . . ."

Axyll Jakubowski looked up to see the door of his suite
sliding silently open, without chimes or alarms or even
any notification from the security office in the lobby.
Moses Callahan, solid and grim-faced, looked back in at
him, while a young man in spacer's togs pulled a key blank
from the lock and disconnected two short lengths of wire
from its edge. For an absurd moment Jakubowski had
been sure the wires were socketed directly into the young
man's arm, but he rolled them up neatly and pocketed the
card without any fuss.

"Mr. Jakubowski," Moses said politely. "You're rather a
difficult man to find."

"That's how I like it," Jakubowski said. "I thought I was
paying enough for the privilege. Whatever the trouble is,
Captain, I'm sure my office could have accommodated
you—"

"I don't think so," Moses disagreed. "Not in the matter
at hand, I'm afraid. It's a question of shedding enough
light on the problem now, you see, as opposed to shedding
entirely too much at some later and less advantageous
date."

Axyll Jakubowski suddenly felt vulnerable and not a
little foolish, standing there barefoot in his pajama bottoms
and potbelly.

"What the hell is this about, Captain?"

"It's about suns, Mr. Jakubowski, sir, and setting them
off inside cities."

"It is . . . I guess you'd better come in, Captain."

"Thank you, sir."

"Sit down, please. Can I get you anything?"

"Under the circumstances, I would think not, thank
you."

"Suit yourself." The hard-base furniture scattered around the room suggested Jakubowski's rough past. No one who'd ever tried to get to his feet in a hurry out of a floater chair ever trusted them again.

"Then in that case, Captain, you may as well come right to the point and tell me what this is all about. Skipping the poetic imagery, if you don't mind."

"To be more specific then, sir: Where did you get a Bethe trigger? What is it doing aboard my ship? And just what do you plan to do with it?"

"Those are three very good questions, Captain," Jakubowski said. "To answer the first, I got it from Fleet. You can't get them anywhere else. Secondly, you're carrying it because I'm paying you good money to carry it. And, finally, I intend to make more good money with it, a whole hell of a lot more."

"Well. I can't say those aren't the answers I expected to hear. Did you expect anything different, Deacon?"

"Not particularly."

"The trouble is, though, Mr. Jakubowski, there's one thing wrong with them—I don't run guns. I never have. And I'm not so bankrupt, either financially or morally, that I'm prepared to start now."

"You don't understand—"

"That's true enough. And I don't propose to let you waste my time trying to enlighten me. Come on, Deacon." Moses stood. "I don't know what you're after, or who's behind you, or how far any of you are prepared to go to get whatever it is, and I'm not hero enough to want to find out. As long as that infernal device stays the hell off my ship you can use it to light a fire under your own arse, as far as I'm concerned. But I want no part of it, or of being your errand boy. Good night, sir."

"You're going to throw away thirty-two thousand standards just like that, huh?"

"I can't afford the trouble they'd buy me."

"Maybe not. But they should buy me an explanation."

"That's your opinion."

"Yeah. Just like it's my opinion that you really don't want to throw away all that money. Do you?"

Moses didn't answer him. But he didn't move.

"Suppose I told you that what I have in mind for the trigger won't hurt a single living soul?"

"I'm happy to hear that. But it seems out of character for the thing somehow."

"And suppose I told you that what I have in mind for the trigger is going to make me so filthy, stinking rich that I don't care how wealthy you get in the process?"

"The best of all possible worlds, to be sure," Moses answered. "That's why I'm so certain there has to be a catch."

"And what if I told you that what I have in mind for the trigger is absolutely legal, as far as you're concerned?" Axyll Jakubowski waited for Moses to answer. Then he grinned. "I thought you'd be interested."

"Whatever your story is," Moses said warily, "it had better be good."

"Good? It's a goddammed epic, Captain, a bloody saga. Sit down, sit down. You sure you and your man don't want those drinks?"

"I think I'm better off indulging just one vice at a time, thank you."

"Whatever you say. Anyhow, the complete, if slightly abridged, story of what somebody like me is doing with an illegal Bethe trigger:

"You probably won't believe this, but I didn't always used to be the class act I am today. I mean, shit, I finished out my last tour with Fleet and I didn't know what the hell I was gonna do for the next sixty years. There isn't all that much demand for middle-aged intrasystem tug pilots with no log time on civilian models, is there?"

"I wouldn't think so," Moses said.

"You wouldn't be wrong. Anyway, I thought about going back to school, getting my ticket updated, but, hell, I was forty-one years old—I was goddammed ancient, right?" He laughed, in rueful self-deprecation. "At least, that was how it felt at the time. But what it came down to was I just couldn't face sitting in some classroom for two or three years just for the privilege of starting out at the bottom all over again. I figured I had better than that coming to me.

"So, I set up a line of credit against my pension, pulled every damn standard I had in the bank out of the bank, and bought my way into a mining partnership."

"Just like that, then?"

"Yeah. Yeah, pretty much just like that, actually. It's never all that hard to find people who aren't satisfied with what they've got. 'Course, if I knew then what I know now . . . Thing is, when you do find 'em, you ought to ask yourself why they don't have more already if they want it so bad."

"You didn't ask."

"Hell, no. But none of them asked about me, either. So I guess that's square all around, isn't it? Anyway, it didn't matter. We were gonna get rich, all of us, even if none of us had ever even seen an asteroid up close before. At least that was the theory."

"It didn't work out that way?"

"Not quite. Like the popcart said, the fault wasn't in the stars, Captain, but in ourselves. Asteroid prospecting's brutal work. You've got to want it, you've got to work at it—and you've got to be ready to sweat it out for a long, long time before it starts to pay off worth a damn. The only trouble with that was that if any of us were capable of that kind of commitment, we probably wouldn't have been available to go prospecting in the first place.

"I think Zhdanov was the first of us to pack it in. I wasn't too surprised, I guess. We never did live up to his high expectations. He had this fancy, idealistic vision of all us noble, cooperative workers hitting the big strike overnight and retiring in well-deserved comfort."

"No, huh?"

"Oh, it was a terrific vision, no complaints there. It's just that actually going out and doing the mining didn't fit into it anywhere. You know what prospecting's like, Captain. You're picking through the garbage dump of the solar system. You take a week to catch up to some lump of rock that's just a dot of light on your screens so you can get a spectro laser on it, and then if it ain't worth shit, which it usually isn't, you turn away around and fly off to another rock another week away and try your luck there. Well, Zhdanov just wasn't up to that. All we could afford was this dumpy old *Atlas*-class tug we rescued from the mothballers, and he just couldn't put up with the crowding and the predigested food and the no privacy and the tempers—hell, you know how it is. It was all just too real for him, I guess.

"Pao left next, and that was a bitch—she was the only

one in the group besides me who had her pilot's ticket. But two or three intrasystem crawls were all she could put up with. I still see her around; she's flying sunrise orbits for the tourists out of Highside; she's doing okay. Then Barnett left, but all he'd brought into the deal was daddy's money, and that was gone, so the hell with him.

"Pacmani tried to stick it out, he really did, but his suit blew a vernier and spun him visor-first into the rim of the airlock, and that was it."

"Jesus."

"Yeah. Messy. It would have put Zhdanov right off his tea and cookies. So that left just me and a half-paid-for tug we'd never even agreed on a name for. A real recipe for success, huh?"

"So what did you do?"

"What did I do? I went out, and when I didn't score big on that run, I reprovisioned as best I could and went out again, and again. It's a drug, prospecting. It hooks you once you start thinking like that. *The next time*, right, the next time, for sure, it's gotta happen. And while you're looking for that next time, you're getting broker and broker. When you finally have to choose between fuel and spare parts, or buying food, you buy the fuel and the parts, and scrape by on the cheapest prepackaged boat rations you can find. And when you get down to choosing between fuel and spares, you choose the fuel, and run on your backups or do without. You'd be amazed at some of the things you don't need to survive out there, Captain, and I hope to god you never have to try and find out just what they are.

"Finally you just stop coming back to the depots at all, unless you've got some little half-junk rock to sell off for a grubstake or you just get sick of the smell of yourself in the air and the taste of yourself in the water. And when you do get back to the depots, they avoid you, because they can see what's going on, and they know you're gonna go out that one time too many and try to shave it too fine that one time too often, and that'll be all. So you start getting strange out there: you start talking to yourself or to people who aren't there, or you don't talk at all, to anybody, and you start to forget what the sound of your voice sounds like.

"That's the kind of shape I was in. I've got good manners, Captain; when I go crazy I at least keep it to myself. But one more trip out, maybe two, and I would have done something stupid enough to be permanent.

"And that's when I found it.

"I thought it was a ship at first, that's how big it was. It threw back a blip like a fifty kiloton liner. My spectro-analysis kit had tracked it months ago, so there wasn't anything to do but go over and check it out by eye.

"It shone, Captain, it gleamed like a giant silver tear-drop just hanging there against the stars. I don't know what quirk of geology let it happen, but I was looking at a fragment of core, pure ore from the heart of whatever planet died to make up the Hybreasil belt. Untainted heavy metals. Hell, nickel-iron looked to be the lightest stuff there—there were veins half a klick wide of stuff we used to bust our humps looking for a few grams of. It was the strike, Captain. The Strike. My own El Dorado.

"And I couldn't do a damned thing with it.

"I cried like a baby. It was just too big. I couldn't maneuver that monster. I could have burned every drop of reaction mass aboard that old tug and it would never have known I was pushing it. I couldn't just break off a chunk and take it back—pure ore like that, everybody would have wanted to know where it came from. I owed too damned much money to let anybody know I had collateral like that floating around. I would have been foreclosed, divvied up, and sold out six different ways before I cleared the surveyor's office. And I wasn't going to stake my claim and then try to sell it to one of the big combines: they would have given me shit for it, a few standards toward another grubstake and sent me on my way, and I wouldn't have been able to turn them down. I couldn't have afforded to. You see my problem? I'd gone from having too little money to having too damned much without ever crossing the ground in between, and it just doesn't work that way."

"So what did you do?"

"I only had one thing working in my favor. That rock was following a crazy down orbit, cutting through the system ecliptic instead of orbiting along it, know what I mean? It was just wild luck that I'd been there to spot it in the first place. So I paced it for a week, to get enough of a track to plot its orbit, so I could find it any time I wanted to in the future.

"Then I went back to the depot and sold out. My ship, my gear, my claims—everything but that one orbit, in my head. I got raped, of course—I hardly got back the ship's value as parts and scrap, but that was what I expected. Thing was, it gave me capital, something to build on.

"I bought my first warehouse twelve years ago, just storage. I wasn't taking any chances back then—I took my few points' safe profit and ran with it, every year. Every standard of it was one more step back out to that rock.

"Then I found my angle. You people, the independents. You came in here, looking for whatever scraps the compradores and the Warrens threw your way, and whatever they offered, you had to take, 'cause you couldn't sit around waiting for something better to turn up. Sitting inport cost you people too much money. So I started acquiring cargoes on spec, small stuff, low profit, stuff the Warrens'd never touch. And when the independents came in, I offered them the charters. I didn't pay as well as the Warrens but I paid a damn sight faster, and I saved you the time and expense of having to scout up your own cargoes."

"It seems to have worked," Moses said, looking around the expensive suite.

"Damn right it did. For the last five years I've been one of the biggest operators outside the Warrens. And I'll tell you something: if I'd thought of this back when I was coming out of the service, I'd probably be a happy man today. But not since I saw that rock. . . . Jesus, every standard I could make in every day of the rest of my life isn't anything compared to what's just floating out there. You can't understand unless you've seen it.

"Anyway, I was almost ready. This was going to be the year, I could liquidate everything and go out and set up a proper claim.

"Then they locked me out. The big mining combines leaned on the Council and set up zones of exclusive exploitation and development out in the belt. Oh, it wasn't restraint of trade, not quite. They were careful to leave zones of open exploration, so the independents couldn't prove they were being squeezed out . . . but my rock fell straight through combine space. I'm out of time. Any day now, one of their prospectors is going to stumble across my find, and then what the hell do I do?"

"You staked your claim, surely. You should be able to get a good deal—"

"You haven't been listening. That's my find. I'm not selling out to anybody. . . . So, fine, I said. If I can't make my claim where the rock is now, I'll just have to put it somewhere that I can."

"And that's why you want the trigger."

"Right. There isn't a tug in the world that could move that thing, and I don't know enough about thrusters or fusion chargers to take a chance on them. But if I can set up a Bethe reaction, I can use it to vaporize enough mass to drive that rock right into the open exploration zone, and claim it there."

"So where did you get the trigger?"

"You ever heard of the League of Humanity?"

"Heard of them?" Deacon said. "I spent a year trying to keep those mad dogs bottled up on Leibensraum."

"Didn't work. You can't lock up an idea with interdiction cutters, no matter how sick it is. Anyway, I couldn't get a trigger myself, but they have people inside Fleet who could. What they needed, that I had, was a way to get the thing off planet quietly."

"So the League thinks they're getting a Bethe trigger."

"Right."

"Aren't they liable to be a little peeved when it never arrives?"

"They won't be in much of a position to do anything about it when I blow the whistle on them to Fleet."

"After you move your precious rock."

"Of course."

"Well," Moses said, "you don't think small. I have to give you that."

"No, I don't, do I? So, are you still in?"

"For thirty-two thousand standards? And a share?"

"And a share. Hell, a point of this deal will net you enough for a fifty-kiloton liner and the bribes to line up a route besides. So, yes or no, Captain?"

"I haven't turned you down."

"Yes or no?"

"Load it as we scheduled."

Jakubowski grinned. "A pleasure doing business with you, sir."

The elevator slid easily down from Jakubowski's suite.
"A pretty little story, wasn't it, Deacon?"
"I thought well of it. Do you buy it?"
"Not a word. I can't afford to."
"Then why are we loading the damned trigger?"
"Because if he isn't lying about the League, I don't want those monsters mad at me for any reason."
"So what are we going to do?"
"We, Mr. Hallorhan, are going to fulfill the absolute letter of our agreement and take this cargo through to Avalon..."
"But it isn't going to Avalon."
"I know. That's why we're going to turn it over to Fleet there."
Deacon grinned. "He can't have both ends covered—"
"Or he wouldn't need us in the middle."
"Very slick."
"I like it."

He wouldn't leave her alone. And he didn't even know it.

Mitsuko's trip to the chandleries had been an ordeal, but an endurable one. The mental noise of the city had swept over her like an arctic gale, cutting, frigid—but finally numbing as well, in much the same manner as frostbitten skin soon becomes insensible to the impact of any individual particle of ice or snow. The very intensity of the onslaught had worked against it, for the short term, reducing the myriad separate impressions rushing in on her to indistinguishable white noise.

But the delivery man was driving her crazy.

It wasn't his fault; she knew that. Even with the limited training she had accepted, she'd learned that the silently shrieking masses around her were not really broadcasting their every stray thought just to drive Mitsuko Tamura crazy—but this one was an expert, and his proximity within the relatively empty port grounds only exacerbated the effect.

He was a nondescript young man, perfectly average,

and that was the horror of it. His undisciplined common-
man's awareness seemed to be composed of nothing but a
twisted stream-of-consciousness progression of song fragments leading into ad jingles leading into snatches of
popcart scenes leading into unconnected snippets of memory setting out faces and encounters Mitsuko had never
experienced before. . . . She looked down at the manifest in
her hands and saw that she had logged in the last carton
three times, misspelling it three different ways. She reversed the cursor and entered it again, correctly, concen-
trating on each letter to block out the image of a fresh-
faced blond promising fast gastric relief to two wounded
spacers lying on a popcart battlefield obscured by hash and
scanning break-up while a fat-faced repairman told them
their modulator head was shot and would have to go back
to the shop. . . .

The image stream thinned briefly as he left the *Goose*'s
cargo lock but it was no respite; he came back again,
staggering under the weight of a crated converter, muscles
straining, mouth moving, adding a running verbal coun-
terpoint to the burgeoning thought-torrent:

"God-damn, ain't this mother heavy, here, where do you
want this *(to the technicolor encephalic tune of older
woman/fresh-faced)* fucker, quick, it's a heavy bitch, where's
it go . . . ?" as he weaved *(popcart starlets/pornicart
sluts/breasts/mouths/tongues/taste/touch/)* across the cluttered
deck—*(small Japanese woman in a cargo lock/cute ass—)*

Mitsuko recoiled, the anger welling up fast and sharp
and momentarily blocking out his thoughts. She acted on
it, automatically, stabbing back into his mind. He never
felt it, was already wandering off down another side-alley
of semisentience, but she brushed through the new wash
of impressions, digging in deeper, into the memories less
easily remembered, on the fringes of the undervoice. She
found what she was looking for.

Perhaps it had been the beer, or the excitement of his
first time, perhaps his own overhigh expectations of himself and the girl. Mitsuko wasn't interested in reasons. She
didn't want to understand him, only to hit back. She dug
in, rooting for the dismayed surprise, the discomfort, the
embarrassment, bringing it out again, suddenly, into the
forefront of his mind. She resurrected the woman's obvi-

ous disappointment and the inferred resentment he had read into her words of understanding. Mitsuko dragged it all out into the light and fixed it there, and the rumble of incoming thought died away into a hurt, confused mumbling.

The delivery man winced as he set down the converter. He avoided Mitsuko's eyes as he signed the hard-copy receipt from the manifest and left without a word, leaving Mitsuko alone with her anger and the sick knowledge of her violence.

"Good morning."

Mitsuko nearly dropped the manifest. She spun around quickly to face the tall, sober-faced young man in the rumpled ship's coverall. A *Wild Goose* crew patch had been sewn to one breast pocket, brighter, newer than the fabric of the faded coverall. "I'm Deke Hallorhan, your new pilot. You must be Mitsuko; Captain Callahan told me about you." She had known him before he spoke, from Moses' memory—but Moses had not, could not, see the impossibility of Deacon Hallorhan.

Mitsuko couldn't hear him. The words came through, clear and audible, but *she couldn't hear him*. There was nothing else, no intruding stream of impressions and memories, no effluential, nigrescent, roiling undervoice that might have warned her of his approach. There were only his words, disturbed air, ill-perceived and tenuous as some poorly learned and half-forgotten foreign language, making no firm connection in her mind.

"Oh," she said finally. "Hello. Yes. Moses told me you'd signed on." *He's a bug, but we need him*, had been Moses' thought as he told her; he didn't know the half of it, she thought. "Do you make a habit of sneaking up on people?"

"Sorry," Hallorhan said. "I don't do it for a living anymore. But you know how it is: old habits and all that bilge." He looked down at her, puzzled by her agitation.

"Don't be put off by Spooky's ways," Moses had said. *"She's good folk, after her fashion. She's just got her quirks, is all."*

*"And I've got mine,"* he'd answered. *"Have you got yours?"*

*He remembered the old captain's grin.* "Enough for the pair of you."

"I'm sorry if I startled you," Hallorhan said.

"Oh, that's all right," Mitsuko said. "I had something on my mind, or something. Please don't worry about it."

"Thanks," Hallorhan said. He studied the stacks of crated stores. "Will she live, doctor?"

"Who—? Oh, the *Goose*—well, as well as ever, I guess. Yes."

"And at her age, too, damn. Listen, I'm no engineer, but if you want a hand, give me a yell. I can't change a light bulb, but I can lift heavy objects real good."

"No, no, I'll be okay, thanks," Mitsuko said, cursing herself silently. She was blithering, babbling into the telepathic silence like smoke dissolving into a vacuum.

*"Dammit, Spooky,"* Moses had once said. *"Did you ever once in your wretched life answer a simple question without sounding like you wanted to talk about something else?"*

She managed a nervous smile for the lanky pilot. "If I didn't have to work too hard I wouldn't have anything to complain about, and then where would I be?"

Hallorhan grinned back. "I'd hate to think. Matter of fact, I'll let you stand my watches too, if you want. Just so you can keep busy."

Mitsuko relaxed slightly, as he accepted her attempt at distancing.

"No, that's okay."

"Just trying to be helpful."

"Thanks anyway." She reached for a carton, the first to hand. "I have to get started if we're going to deliver this trigger of yours."

"The captain told you?"

"There aren't a lot of secrets aboard this ship." Just the one, she thought—and now his.

Why couldn't she *hear* him?

"It doesn't seem to worry you," Hallorhan said.

"I worry about things I can fix." She hefted the carton. "Engines, I can fix."

Hallorhan stared at the carton's label. "With cabin head gasket seals?"

Mitsuko forced herself not to look at the prop that had

betrayed her. "Yes, well, I know what this old tub is good for, don't I?"

"You ought to," Hallorhan admitted, but his agreement fell into the void of his impossible telepathic silence, and left no impression.

# CHAPTER 4

It was going to happen, Jakubowski thought. He was going to do it.

He jumped heavily down off the ramp of the flatbed hauler and looked back at the crated Bethe trigger, lashed fast in its tie-downs. It had taken seventeen years, but he was ready. Everything was.

He had stared at the trigger for what seemed like hours before closing up its crate for the last time.

But now it was time to move it out. Jakubowski slammed the gate of the hauler shut and looked at his watch. The League agent working out of Fleet Security was late, and Jakubowski did not want to move the trigger to the *Wild Goose* without him.

He left the hauler and crossed to the loading-dock door. Warm daylight divided the warehouse floor into twin rectangles of shadow as he slid them open and stepped through.

It is a characteristic of modern weapons that outside of popcarts and similar entertainments, they are effectively silent. Jakubowski had never heard the shot that took the agent and dropped him in the driveway, to lie there ungainly and awkward in his ill-fitting civilian clothes.

And he never heard the shot that pierced his spine between the shoulder blades and killed him. He never heard, let alone saw, his killer. All he heard, as the last fragments of life and consciousness fled him, as he lay face down on the concrete driveway staring at its gritty surface millimeters from his eyes, was the distant laughter that seemed to come in some strange way from someplace deep in the back of his head. . . .

"We're liable to miss him like this," Hallorhan said. The sled wallowed on its fans as Moses Callahan tried to thread it through the crowded traffic.

"We've missed him already," Callahan said. "He should have been at the *Goose* two hours ago." He looked around carefully for any sign of a traffic monitor, then fed power to the fans and blipped the sled over and beyond a double-parked hauler. "If the man's going to make a hardened criminal out of me, he can at least be punctual about it."

"Suppose he shows up while we're out here looking for him?" Hallorhan flinched as a stream of traffic followed them over the hauler and sped past them on three sides.

"Then Spooky'll let him in. She'll probably lock herself in on the bridge, but she'll let him in. How much farther?"

"Next right."

Callahan turned the corner, and started to back-fan frantically. "Jesus Christ—"

"Don't slow down," Hallorhan said quietly. "Just go on by."

They cruised down the warehouse block, little improved by daylight, toward the cluster of police cruisers and emergency vehicles.

"Dammit," Callahan said. "Is that his place?"

"That's his place," Hallorhan said. "Just keep driving. Nothing to do with us, Captain."

A bored cop waved at them with paired traffic batons, directing them around the clustered vehicles. They slid past. A body-bagged figure could be seen, briefly, between the grounded vehicles and milling experts, stretched out in the driveway. Then the view was obscured again by the waiting ambulance and the knots of pedestrian onlookers.

Several blocks away, Callahan grounded the sled and dropped the controls.

"Dammit," he said again, pounding the heel of his palm on the dash. "Dammit, dammit, dammit. That had to have something to do with us, of course."

"Probably," Hallorhan said.

"Do you think they know about the damned trigger? Do you think they know about us?"

"You want to go back and ask?"

"Not bloody likely. What the hell do we do now?"

"Go back to the ship."

"And what if they know about us?"

"What are they going to do about it? You signed to ship a cargo for Jakubowski, Captain, that's all."

"A thirty-two thousand standard deal for one cargo?"

"It was important to him. What the hell did you care why? You'd do better to wonder whether or not he paid you up with the port before he went down."

"Shit." Callahan's frown deepened; another hitch added to the noose. "Well, hell, we aren't going anywhere anyway until Spooky gets the drive put back together. Let's go give her the good news."

Mitsuko sat back heavily from the access port with the thirty-kilogram feeder relay propped across her thighs. It was an awkward position to work in, but damned if she was going to lug that monster all the way back to the workbench. She selected a thick Allen wrench from the toolboxes scattered around her and bent forward to undo the cover plate.

Then she looked up and saw the library around her.

"Fuck," she said clearly.

"I'm afraid that's not at all feasible," Eisberg said. "We do have our limits, you know."

Mitsuko sat there in the plush acrebeast carpet, staring at the glossily varnished Kassen's-oak shelves and paneling, the shelves loaded with thick old books, real books, owned and read as much because they were the sort of things one *should* own and read as for any merit they possessed on their own, and the chunky feeder relay in her lap looked grossly out of place. She gripped it tightly, reassuring herself with its reality.

She hitched around clumsily, rubbing a swath in the pile of the carpet. Eisberg sat there in the Edwardian armchair, just as cool and blond and ever-so-perfect as she remembered him, not a wrinkle in his cravat or a crease in his pants leg out of place.

"This is a new one," she said.

"To you perhaps," Eisberg said. "But you must have noticed by now that your—premature—departure has left the most regrettable lacunae in your education."

"I manage," she said.

"I'm sure you do," Eisberg agreed. "The universe doubtless has desperate need of telepathic mechanics. Or do you still try to ignore your gift?"

"How are you doing this?"

"Odd. From your fiery little resignation speech, I would not have expected you to be curious."

"I'm not. But I have work to do, and if I don't give you a chance to show me how clever you are, you'll keep this up all day. How the hell did you find me out here?"

"But I know how clever I am, and you did, after all, decline the bulk of what we chose to offer you. I think it is sufficient simply to assure you that the mechanics of nodal sentience are sufficient to the situation at hand."

"Nodal—then you're not on Hybreasil."

Eisberg frowned slightly. "Certainly not. Whatever for?"

"You can't reach this far. Nobody can."

"Dear little Mitsuko, I can reach as far as my carrier can afford to take ship. Oh, you needn't worry, he's being well paid for his travels, and the nodes are not likely to have any adverse effect on his base sentience, such as it is."

"I'm happy to hear that. Does he know he's running around with little chunks of you in his head?"

"Oh, well, that would be an unnecessary complication, wouldn't it? To say nothing of being just too naively trusting."

She shook her head. "You bastards. You haven't changed."

"Why should we?"

"How did you find me?"

"You've asked that already."

"I'll keep asking. I've got time, I'm here. How long will that node of yours maintain?"

"As long as is needful. But very well. The Annexes are very good at keeping track of our membership, even the more wayward truants. We've known where to find you since Proxima Wentworth."

"That was six years ago. Why come after me now?"

"Because the time has come for a return on our investment."

"I owe you nothing," Mitsuko said.

"You owe us everything you are. You owe us your sanity, you owe us your life, you owe us most of all your gift."

"My gift." Absently, she slapped the hard alloy of the

feeder relay. "That's beautiful. You want it back, it's yours. I promise I won't miss it."

"Wouldn't you? After all the good use you've got from it?" He smiled; he knew, damn him. "Of course you have. All those little things, and just-onces, and unfortunate necessities? You haven't changed either, you know. You still won't admit the rules are different for such as us."

"Are they?"

"Of course they are. Because we have the gift, we have the talent. You wouldn't ask one of the mundanes to voluntarily do without his sight or his hearing, would you? We owe it to ourselves to use our natural abilities to the fullest. It's simple masochism to think otherwise."

"I won't be a parasite."

"Such a waste," Eisberg said. "All that wonderful thinking being done out there—why won't you take advantage of it? Take my case, for one—I've just discovered this absolutely brilliant market analyst; she can call trading futures like fine clockwork. Why shouldn't I benefit from it? What harm does it do her?"

"What good does she get from your picking her brains?"

"But I don't. You never understood that. She's doing all that excellent thinking anyway; if she should do it where and when I happen to be looking for it, why shouldn't I consider it public domain?"

"You're a leech, Eisberg. I prefer to pay my own way."

"Yes." He beamed paternally. "And look how well you're doing."

"Oh, piss off. What do you want from me?"

"I'm afraid your Institute requires one last service from you."

"I'm finished with the Institute."

"But we're not finished with you."

"So what?"

"So unless you can see your way clear to cooperating with us, we might have to inform the appropriate authorities that they have one of those near-mythical telepaths wandering around their frontiers."

"And five minutes after they come for me, they'll know everything about the Institute I can think of to tell them."

"Which will do you how much good?" Eisberg asked. "We're very good at taking care of one another, don't forget that. We've been at it for a very long time. But you're out here all alone."

"What's this service?" Mitsuko asked, finally.

"Ah. Good. Well, it seems there's a small problem out your way. There seems to be another free spirit on the loose out there."

"Another telepath?"

"Exactly so."

"And not the Institute's?"

"Again, so."

"Great. More power to him."

"I'm afraid it's not quite that simple."

"Isn't it?"

"No. You see, whereas we seem to be, in your terms, some kind of parasite, he's something of a carnivore."

"That bad?"

"He frightens us. And you must admit, very little does." Eisberg frowned. "We observe. He controls."

"So what do you need a dropout like me for? Let your Annex handle it."

"Why should we expose our Annex when we have you so conveniently to hand? The whole point of the matter is that we would like to deal with this fellow before he calls too much attention to our kind. And you shall be our instrument."

"You're sure of that, are you?"

"Oh, yes. Because I'll be there to watch."

The deck was cold metal under her again. Mitsuko sat there for a moment, and then picked up the Allen wrench and went back to work.

He paused to watch the lighter stabbing skyward on the port's laser track, and for a moment he was almost whole again.

It happened that way every time. He would watch the ships climbing out, or a world falling away beneath him, or even something as commonplace as young ship's crews boiling out of their docking complexes in a bubbling liberty rush, and Luther Orange would almost make it back, back to the self and soul he had inhabited when Captain Luther Orange and the *Boyne* both had been going concerns. But he would never get there again, and he knew it. *Boyne* was gone, her notes having overtaken her, broken up for scrap or leased onto a no-loss loop run by the damned bank; it was all the same to Luther because he wasn't aboard her and she wasn't his, never again. His old self was lost in an accretion of fine clothes and fat cashplates, and his soul, well, Luther Orange knew he'd let *that* go years before, when he first agreed to let that cold, quiet voice move into the back of his head and take up tenancy.

*Tenancy?* the thought came, with the sneering, superior note in it Luther had learned to hate even as his mind cringed from it. *Isn't that understating the relationship, "Captain?" Reversing it, actually. Seneschal, perhaps, would be closer to the mark. Or viceroy. Or possibly merely concierge, looking after the property for the less capable tenants. . . .*

"All right," Luther said aloud. The sound of his voice reassured him. It never changed anything, but it reassured him. "Whatever you want."

*Of course, "Captain." As always.*

"Damn you, White—"

*If you feel you must. Although as long as you're willing to work for me, as long as you'll obey me—as long as you'll seduce and corrupt and kill for me—I really don't need your approval, "Captain." Merely your hands. You know, that's even more descriptive of our relationship than concierge. "Hands." Yes. I like it.*

"Stop it," Luther said, too loudly. The couple standing nearby looked at him and moved away nervously.

*You have an appointment,* the voice reminded him.

"I know."

*Then you had better be on your way. I'd hate to have to tell myself you were tardy when we get home.*

The voice was blessedly silent during the cab ride, as they floated swiftly through the warehouse district. Luther would not have wanted to risk its goading him into an outburst in front of the driver. There was no telling what it might have done to the poor bastard if he had taken alarm.

He stepped down from the cab a block and a half from his destination, one of the warehouses on the very edge of the district, bordering the farthest empty reaches of the port grounds.

Nullman was waiting for him in the seedy lunchroom, perspiration streaking his balding head as he laboriously struggled with his oversize luggage. Nullman looked up as Luther entered, and the voice let him feel the man's spark of excitement, still high after the killings. The voice had fastened on him on the voyage out principally because of the small handgun he already owned. It would have been a convenience not to have to rely on obtaining a weapon if the voice should desire one during the voyage. But Nullman turned out to possess treasures far beyond his cheap little pistol. He was a positive morass of inhibitions, suppressed angers, repressed desires, fuming submerged intimations of impotence, that the voice shared with Luther in loving detail as it uncovered them layer by layer on the trip from Avalon. It should have expected as much, the voice told him, even before it probed, from the dowdy wife and the fact that a middle-echelon Western Galactic accounting tech was taking his twenty-five years' bonus as a working passage in *Western Ranger*'s Purser's Office and from his desire for the weapon in the first place. Even before it had needed the man, the voice had found him endlessly entertaining, poking and prodding—the dowdy wife wondered why her husband had grown so temperamental and erratic, and masked her alarm under a deeper layer of astringent nagging—or simply wandering about in the dark cellars of Nullman's mind, enjoying the lurid fantasies the little clerk walked through every day.

"You disposed of League man's body?" Luther asked.

"Of course, Captain, just like you said," Nullman said eagerly.

"I'm no captain," Luther said.

"Once a captain, always a—"

"Drop it," Luther said. It was an hour later than Nullman had promised his wife he'd return to *Western Ranger*, the voice told him gleefully. *He's having the argument already. It's wonderful, better than a popcart melodrama. He's so aggressive. So forceful. The shouting, the throwing things, the slap. It's a shame it will never happen that way. She'd break his arms. Unless I help him. Should I do that, loyal hands? Should I help his dream come true for once? After all, it will be his last chance . . . yes. Yes, I will. What use is a toy one doesn't play with?*

Luther shrugged.

"Good luck," he said, and stared back at the perplexed Nullman.

# CHAPTER 5

"I hate this," Callahan said. "I truly do." The warmth of the early morning sunlight streaming in through the open cargo lock was a great, soft weight upon his shoulders, exacerbating the weariness of a sleepless, nervous night. He imagined he saw his exhaustion mirrored in Hallorhan's drawn face, but then he had never seen Hallorhan look any other way.

"Like I said, Captain," Hallorhan answered, "I don't think there's a hell of a lot you can do about it."

"You did say that, didn't you?" Moses grumbled. "Seems that's the only thing you can say."

"When it's right, Captain."

"Right or not, we can't just stand here—"

"That's the only thing we can do. Look, Jakubowski's deal has gone sour, but so far that doesn't involve us. We're just the people who agreed to carry a cargo for Outward Bound. That's our only connection to the whole mess, and that's how we want to keep it. But if we start poking around, asking questions and bothering people, we're only going to draw attention to ourselves. We don't know who killed Jakubowski, if that was him in the bag. It could have been Fleet, it could have been the League, it could have been somebody we don't know about. And we don't know how we stand with any of them. So let's just sit tight and see what happens."

"No," Moses said. "What we'll do, we'll wait until the delivery is past due on board, then we'll call Outward Bound and ask them what's happened to it. There can't be anything suspicious in that, can there?"

"I don't see how," Hallorhan said. "Might even look funny if we didn't check up then."

The inner lock cycled open behind them. Mitsuko stood there, the rim of the hatch between herself and the two men.

"We're clear with port finance," she said. "Whatever else is going on, no one's thought to cancel our credit yet."

"That all they said?" Hallorhan asked.

Mitsuko shrugged. "The readout on our account had a flag through to an article about the shooting yesterday. It was Jakubowski," she expanded, and Moses shut his mouth, his question forestalled. "They know we're carrying his cargo, but then they already knew that."

"It won't make any difference to them unless the shipment's canceled," Moses said. "As long as we can pay, they don't care whose funeral we go to."

"So all we have to do now is wait and see if the damned thing shows up."

"No, we won't," Mitsuko said, but they could already see for themselves the van gliding across the field toward the *Goose* . . . and the passenger bus following close behind.

"What the hell is this?" Moses asked. Hallorhan could only shrug.

The hauler settled on its fans at the lip of the slip, its flatbed stacked with cargo pallets. The bus eased in under the overhang of the *Wild Goose*, turbines roaring shrilly in the narrow space between hull and slip wall.

The two men who dismounted were strangers to them all, the port officer escorting them a brisk distillation of all the crisp, efficient young men and women who had ever given Moses Callahan grief from behind the security of a rule book and a steady paycheck.

Luther Orange was the first man up the ramp, white-haired, clear-eyed, imposing and robust, impeccably tailored: a Moses Callahan who had made good. But it was his other face, the stranger's eyes that looked back at her through his, that held Mitsuko's stare, held her and terrified her even as Luther turned away. They were heavy-lidded windows onto a dissipated soul, framed in a fleshy sensualist's face, underscored by a cruel, full mouth that might register gratification but never pleasure, and they shone with a radiant, unfettered appetite that appalled her.

She wanted to run, to bolt back into the familiar safe depths of the ship, away from the hunger she saw in those eyes and her helplessness to warn Moses of its approach. But she could only stand there and watch as Luther and his doppelganger made their way up to the hatch.

"Maddening, isn't it?" Suddenly Eisberg was there beside her, appearing with all the abrupt solidity of any apparition in a nightmare. Mitsuko made herself face away from him, kept her eyes on the approaching men. "Meet our carnivore, my dear—or at least his avatar."

"Who the hell is that?" she thought back, deluding herself that she kept most of the fear out of the thought.

"The meat is Captain Luther Orange," Eisberg said, "formerly of the independent commercial carrier *Boyne*. He has since found somewhat less independent employment. But the gentleman I believe you are referring to is Mr. James Emerson White—or rather, a nodality of the same. Personable sort, isn't he?"

"Looks absolutely charming."

"Actually, however, he is quite a monster, by any standards—even ours. And do you know the most monstrous thing about him, as far as you're concerned?"

"I'm sure you'll tell me."

"Of course. The most monstrous thing about James Emerson White is that there isn't one single thing you can do about him."

"You still haven't convinced me I should want to," she thought back.

"Simply consider that face once more."

"Do I have a choice?"

"What do you see there?" Eisberg pressed. "Greed? Cruelty? Self-indulgence? Not a very likeable combination, is it?"

"No," Mitsuko agreed. "You should be very happy together."

"How droll. But he is possessed of a further quality you should find less amusing."

"And what's that?"

"Knowledge. He knows about your cargo."

"Just like you seem to."

"Of course I do. After all, *you* do."

"Then you know people are dying because of it."

"People aren't my concern. But he's boarding your ship; you might have cause to worry."

"Thank you for the advice."

"The question now becomes, however, what are you going to do about it?"

"All right, what?"

"Nothing at all. There isn't anything a half-trained telepathic mechanic can do, under the circumstances."

"I could warn them."

"About what? That they have a manifestation of a homicidal telepath coming on board to steal their illegal cargo? And how would you tell them you found this out?"

"I don't have to *tell* them anything."

"Certainly not. I only thought you were above such crude manipulation."

"You go to hell." She turned her attention away from the smug nodality to Moses Callahan. Even without trying, she could feel his growing unease at the presence of two strangers when he had seemed so nearly free and clear. She followed that discomfort inward, shaping an image of Axyll Jakubowski and Luther Orange, overlaying it with impressions of blood and violence, a body bag full and zippered in a driveway under flashing police lights, Luther brandishing a large and menacing handgun—

Then the heavy, corrupt face of James Emerson White was looming up before her, a smile of assured power shaping its features. Beyond it the images Mitsuko had so carefully assembled froze and blurred, wrenched from her control. She fought forward, trying to regain them, sharpening edges, heightening contrasts, as White plucked the handgun from Luther Orange's unresisting fingers and tossed it aside, out of existence, and in the same movement whirled to slap her stingingly across the face—

Moses stood in the hatchway, oblivious to the skirmish fought and lost on the border of his mind. And the White nodality grinned at her from the eyes of its bearer, a grin broadened by the knowledge of its success. Mitsuko turned and retreated into the *Goose*.

"I did warn you," Eisberg said, almost sympathetically.

"I thought you said he'd never had any training."

"Not a day—he's entirely a self-made man."

"I can't do anything like that."

"You couldn't survive without the Institute's training, either. He has. Whatever else you may say of him, he is strong."

"Stronger than I am." The nodality didn't respond. "So what do you expect me to do about him?"

"On your own, nothing. But with the further training I can offer you—"

"No."

"You misunderstand your situation. White's agent is going to board your ship. You cannot prevent that. Your only chance to deal with it is to accept what I can teach you."

"I've had two years of your personal tutoring already, remember?"

"From which you learned precious little," the nodality rebuked her sharply. "Just because you've managed to avoid going insane doesn't mean you've mastered even the least aspect of your talent. But now you have no choice in the matter."

"Of course not," Mitsuko thought bitterly. "No one ever has any choice in the matter when you want something, do they?"

"In this case, what I want is something you need. Accept that."

"I can't refuse it, can I? So let's not pretend you're doing me any favors. When's your carrier coming aboard?"

"He won't be," Eisberg answered. "All that is required for our purpose is a subject and an instructional nodality. You. Myself. A second repository for the nodality is unnecessary."

"A second repository—no," she said, the familiar, helpless anger rising behind her voice. "*No*."

But she was protesting to silence, a silence in which she was no longer alone.

Moses felt the inner seal ram home as Mitsuko fled the airlock. He had expected as much; the strangers and the port officer were at the outer hatch.

"Captain Callahan." The port officer made it a statement rather than a question, looking straight at him, and the manner in which he said it made clear that Moses had fulfilled his very worst expectations. "Permission to come aboard, sir." And that didn't sound like a request.

"Come aboard." Moses stood aside to allow the three men into the lock, which began to seem far too crowded for comfort.

"You're lifting out today, aren't you, Captain?"

"I'm scheduled for fourteen hundred hours, that's right, yes."

"And your next port of call is Balm, on Avalon."

"The same."

"You're not carrying any passengers."

"No. Strictly a cargo charter." He looked at the two men. "At least, it was going to be."

"Captain Orange and Mr. Nullman are seeking passage to Avalon, Captain. They made application to Mission House when they found no carriers listed for that direction."

"Well, no, they wouldn't have. This flight's basically a private charter for Outward Bound. Did they try approaching the company?"

"Outward Bound informs us that your charter with them merely covers freight haulage. Passenger bookings were left to the discretion of the ship master."

"That's as may be," Moses said. "I've got cabin space, but a Wander Bird's no liner. I hadn't thought to offer any passages."

"Perhaps you didn't, Captain. But there are no other ships lifting out for Avalon in the immediate future. I'm sure I don't have to quote the relevant passages of the Commerce Facilitation Acts to you." He sounded as though he would have liked to, though.

"'In due recognition of the unique exigencies and strictures inherent in interstellar transport and travel, no master shall refuse a lawful request for passage under any reasonable circumstances, save where a demonstrable hazard to vessel or crew may be deemed to exist.'"

"You've heard it before, Captain."

"A time or two. And they've made a lawful request, have they?"

"To a previously declared port of call, with cabin space available, and the approval of Mission House, yes."

"Yes." Moses looked to Luther Orange. "I don't suppose you'd consider yourself a demonstrable hazard."

"I've never thought so, Captain." But Moses noticed the minute change in the balding little man's—Nullman's—expression. The little butterball actually thought he *was* a hard case, he realized.

"I can't promise you anything lavish," Moses warned. "You'll have a berth and meals, and you'll eat what we eat."

"I understand, Captain," Luther Orange said. "I signed my first articles in a Wander Bird."

"Of course, that was back before he made something of himself," Nullman said.

"Of course it was," Moses said levelly, ignoring the gibe. Nullman stared at him, waiting for the reaction he knew his wit must inspire. When it was not forthcoming, he turned his gaze on Hallorhan, who responded with an unfeigned disinterest.

"Then you'll take them aboard," the port officer said.

"It's the law," Nullman reminded him instantly.

"As the man says, it is the law," Moses said. "I suppose I'm obliged."

"Fine. Then if you'll just collect their luggage from the bus, I'll be on my way."

It was some satisfaction to Moses that Luther Orange shared his annoyance with the young swine.

"Wander Birds don't carry too many stewards as a rule, officer. I think Mr. Nullman and I can manage our own kit."

"As I said," Moses reminded them, "the *Goose* is no liner."

"Not to worry, Captain," Luther Orange smiled. "This is going to be like coming home."

Hallorhan ducked through the low hatch and slipped his bony length into the pilot's station. "They're all settled in, Captain. I put Captain Orange in cabin four and Nullman in three."

"One might think you didn't trust them," Moses said. Three and four were the portside cabins, and could be cut off completely from any of the ship's service areas.

"One just might. I took this off Nullman." Hallorhan leaned over the rim of his station and stretched out a hand. It held a gleaming pocket laser.

"I'll stow it away," Moses said, accepting it. "Our Mr. Nullman is shaping up to be quite a jewel."

"Isn't he, though? He looked like I'd kicked a leg out from under him when I took his little toy away."

"He didn't want to give it up, did he?"

"I sort of forgot to ask. Ruined the cut of his jacket, anyway." Hallorhan turned to study the board in front of him.

"That's a standard BuShips layout," Moses said. "Any problems?"

"No, I can manage it, no trouble. You've got a lot of yellow-status systems, though."

"You should have seen it before Spooky fixed it up."

"I hear that. No problem, I've flown yellow before. Is the lady going to be joining us?"

"Not likely. You'll be lucky if you see her before Avalon."

"I guess she likes her privacy."

"She'll never admit it. To hear her tell it, she's back there holding this old bitch together with bare hands and baling wire. You about ready?"

"All set here. Anytime you want." Hallorhan leaned forward and unlocked the atmospheric-flight yoke. Moses keyed open the intercom.

"Wind her up, Spooky."

Deep in the stern of the ship, Mitsuko opened her own mike and answered the familiar call.

"Ready here, Moses. We've got a green board for atmospherics. Open ducts. Maximum venturi choke. All fans running smooth."

As she spoke she was keying in command after command to the drives. Behind and beneath her, the unbroken tube of the main drive outlet contracted, a narrow band dividing the uniform cylinder into two chambers separated by a narrow wasp waist. Vents opened into the innermost chamber as the great air intakes on the outer hull slatted open, steel whales' mouths seeking to strain the thin air soup around them down their broad gullets. Above her, the ducted fans began to keen, their shrill ferocity muted by the thick insulation of their housings.

"You've got drive," she announced.

"Thank you," Moses said, and keyed up the port frequency. "Hybreasil groundside, this is ICC *Wild Goose*, bound outsystem and requesting clearance." He couldn't help grinning as he said it; it was the phrase that summed up everything parochial little Og Eirrin had lacked for a much younger man not yet dead.

"*Wild Goose, this is Hybreasil groundside confirming your window at one four zero zero hours. Clearance granted. Winds from local northeast at seven point two kilometers per. Use runway two.*"

"Understood, groundside. Will comply."

"*Go with God, Captain.*"

"Amen, groundside. *Wild Goose*, out." Deep within the bones of the old tramp Moses could feel the inaudible vibration of the turbines and the freedom they promised. "Roll her out, Mr. Hallorhan."

"Aye, aye, sir."

Hallorhan slowly fed power to the fans. Slowly, but with a ponderous grace not to be overlooked, the *Wild Goose* eased ahead, rolling gently forward out of her slip.

The nimble little utility van cut across her bows and turned ahead of the ship, the traditional black and yellow FOLLOW ME sign flashing. Hallorhan leaned into the control yoke and the elderly freighter swung in line behind its guide.

The runway was a bar-straight line across the landscape, arrowing out into an unfettered horizon. Hallorhan's eyes were down on the board in front of him, watching the displays validate system after system and the chronometer flickering through the final seconds of their groundside confinement. There was nothing for Moses Callahan to do but sit back and watch the scenery.

"Coming up on fourteen hundred hours, mark," Hallorhan said. "Rolling out."

The fans shrilled with new vigor and the *Wild Goose* began to accelerate down the runway. A new undertone was added to the vibration of the hull, the rumble of wheels over permaplast, the sharper jolts of shocks transmitted through the undercarriage suspension.

The *Wild Goose* surged ahead, too big to seem to be gathering any great speed. But the readout in front of Hallorhan recorded her swift acceleration, and already the air cleft by her blunt airfoil hull sought to heal the rift caused by her passage, pressing against her smooth belly, driving the great mass of her upward with ever-increasing vigor.

"Vee one," Hallorhan announced, as the nosewheel lifted gently free of the ground; then, "vee two."

The vibration of the landing gear vanished. There was a slight sensation of sagging, and then renewed motion as the *Wild Goose* lifted free of the imprisoning earth beneath it.

"Hybreasil groundside, ICC *Wild Goose* is airborne," Moses announced.

"Acknowledged, *Wild Goose*. Come to magnetic heading two six three and maintain angle of climb."

"Understood, groundside."

The *Wild Goose* climbed steadily into the deepening blue of the Hybreasil sky, leaving behind land-bound entanglements and even the sound of its own passing. The sky beyond the viewports darkened further: navy, royal purple. The horizon line thickened with a band of denser atmosphere marking the curvature of the planet beneath them.

"Coming up on thirty thousand meters," Hallorhan announced. Through the clouds below, the brown crust of a coastline appeared as the ship drove out over untenanted ocean.

"Wild Goose, *this is Hybreasil groundside. We show you as good for primary ignition.*"

"Thank you, groundside," Moses said. "We'll switch over at thirty-five thousand. Spooky, you hear that?"

Mitsuko leaned forward into her console again. "Right, Captain. Inertial stabilizers on line, drive ready for transition."

"Thirty-four thousand," Hallorhan said. "Switching over to inertials." The external maneuvering surfaces, their effect fading rapidly in the diminished atmosphere surrounding the ship, closed back flush with the hull as the inertial stabilizers hummed up to speed at the freighter's center of mass. The yoke under Hallorhan's hands moved with a new authority as the stabilizers provided a fresh base of resistance to maneuver against.

"Thirty-five thousand."

"Transition," Moses ordered. "Cut fans."

In the engine room, Mitsuko worked her keyboard. "Gravitics up," she announced, feeding power to the elderly fixed-plane systems. "Cutting fans now." The distant whine of the ducted fans faded away. The *Wild Goose* continued to arc upward on momentum alone now, the internal gravitics maintaining its inhabitants' weight. "Losing the venturi." The main drive outlet straightened again, the inlet ducts closing off and restoring the outlet's mirror-smooth interior. "Outlet clear and ready."

"Fire main," Moses ordered.

Deep in the heat of the worn, ancient freighter, a perfect thing was born. Power flowed from the squat fusion reactor to the drive, to be released as pure photonic energy, light, collimated into a solid bar of driving power. The *Wild Goose* leaped forward with a vigor cushioned by her internal gravitics, while the far end of her drive emission, little defused by twenty miles of atmosphere, gouged steam from the face of the sea beneath it.

"Main engaged and optimal, good transition," Hallorhan said. "On course and climbing out."

"Looks like we're going to get away with it," Moses said.

"We got away with leaving," Hallorhan said. "We still have to get away with coming down again."

"Don't you ever get tired of injecting so much sunshine into people's lives?"

"Once in a while," Hallorhan admitted.

"Everything in order, Spooky?" Moses asked.

"The ship's doing fine, Captain."

"I'll settle for that," Moses said. He turned back to Hallorhan. "There's nothing to be done now 'til the first correction. Who wants the first watch?"

"I'll take it," Hallorhan said indifferently. "Why don't you go see how our passengers are doing?"

"That's a good thought, isn't it?"

The engine room was quieter now. The ducted fans were silent and would remain so until called upon at planetfall. The main fusion plant itself was sealed away behind its massive cladding, as impervious to sound as to rampaging neutrons. And the drive itself, save for the occasional chime of an indicator, was as noiseless as a beam of sunshine. There was only the muted whirring of the ventilation fans and the sound of Mitsuko's own voice, her immediate duties completed and no distraction from her horror as she stared unseeing at the board before her.

"Get out," she said softly, as though to herself. "Get out, get out, get *out*."

But there was no answer, save for the faintest whisper of a ghost laughter not her own, fleeting, mocking, elusive, fading in the depths of her mind.

The *Wild Goose* boasted no lounge as such; it would have been considered an unconscionable waste of space not even to be considered in the poorer, less sophisticated days of her youth. So the crew's wardroom/gym was forced to do double duty.

Orange and Nullman were there already, and had unfolded several sections of hinged table down from the bulkhead.

"I believe congratulations are in order, Captain," Luther Orange said. "That was a very smooth takeoff."

"Thank you, Captain. I see you remember your way around these old ladies."

"That's the one thing I've made sure of in my long career," Luther Orange said. "I may not be able to find the flight deck, the lifeboats or my backside with both hands, but I can always find the bar. Only sometimes I get there and the sadists aren't open."

"Scandalous," Moses said, switching on the food and drink processors. "I wouldn't stand for it, myself."

"Nor would I, in my day. After all, you don't have to drink to master your own vessel—"

"—but by God, it helps," Moses finished for him. "What'll you take?"

"What have you got?"

Moses made a show of studying the board. "Something that calls itself whiskey, something that calls itself rum, and something that calls itself a lager."

"And what do you call them?"

"Better than nothing."

"I'll take a chance on a whiskey, neat, thank you."

"And you, Mr. Nullman?"

"I don't suppose you have any wine."

"I've always thought that was a terrible thing to do to a defenseless grape, but I imagine I can dial up something that isn't violently offensive."

"Please."

"Here you go, then—carefully trodden by little cybernetic feet."

"Thank you."

Moses swung a chair-bottom down from the bulkhead and settled himself across from them. "It will be quite some time yet before we've built up enough of a base-line course to shift from," he said. "I'm afraid we don't boast much in the way of recreational facilities. There are a few popcarts on board somewhere; you're welcome to make use of them as you please."

"Much obliged," Luther Orange said.

"Or we could pass the time more profitably, in genteel conversation, if you'd rather. For instance, we could discuss why you felt you had to rope the port authorities in on me before you even asked after passage."

"Yes, that was a bit heavy-handed of me, wasn't it," Luther Orange said. "I suppose I should apologize. I would never have put up with it in my day."

"But you asked me to put up with it, didn't you?"

"I'm afraid it was necessary, Captain."

"Was it, now?"

"It was. I've business on Avalon that requires my immediate attention. I couldn't afford any sort of delay."

"And what sort of business is that?"

"There's a shipment en route to my employers that I have to be there to receive."

There was a sudden, coppery taste at the back of Moses' throat.

"Is there?"

Luther Orange nodded. "Industrial electronics. It's a new prototype system, a whole grade above anything produced locally." He looked at Moses. "It should have quite an impact."

"I expect it will. Is there some reason you thought I might take exception to that?"

Luther Orange shrugged. "Why take the chance when I didn't have to, Captain?"

"Of course."

"Do you think I'll be able to access my consignment on board, if I have to?"

"I don't see why that should be necessary."

"Well, this is a revolutionary system, Captain. My employers are naturally concerned about its welfare."

"Oh, naturally. But I'd prefer not to breach my seals before customs."

"Fair enough. I can understand that. We'll discuss the matter again, perhaps."

"I don't see that there's a whole lot to discuss, Captain Orange. This is my ship. I've made my wishes known."

"Certainly, Captain," Luther Orange conceded. But it was not a surrender. "I meant no imposition. But it may be worthwhile to reopen the discussion at another time, under different circumstances."

"Well," Moses said, "we'll cross that bridge when it's burning behind us."

"So why are you surprised, Captain?" Hallorhan asked. "These two show up the morning we're due to lift out, carrying a midnight cargo and hoping to avoid a murder investigation. They tell you they're taking passage and hit you over the head with Mission House to prove it before you even have a chance to make a fuss—you can't be surprised they're mixed up with Jakubowski's crowd."

"No, of course not, you're right," Moses said, "but—"

"But 'what are we going to do about it?' You aren't going to like this, Captain—"

"You're going to tell me there's nothing we can do, again, aren't you?" Moses said wearily. "Do you know, I'm getting used to the sound of that? Now tell me why we can't."

"Because for once, we haven't got a problem," Hallorhan explained. "There's only two of them, and if they have any weapons besides Nullman's popgun, the security programs haven't turned them up."

"Checked that, did you?"

"Sure."

"I would have eventually, I suppose. . . ."

"We have them quartered where they can't get at the trigger or at any vital systems, and if they try to program access through any terminal on board, we'll know it. All we have to do is keep an eye on them. They're on your ship now, Captain. They have to play our game, and this time the advantage is ours."

"I imagine you're right," Moses said. "As long as we're playing the game we think we are. . . ."

# CHAPTER 6

The sun beat down brightly on the sawdust-filled pit, its timbered perimeter packed tight with anonymous, shaven-headed trainees. Sweat already darkened the armpits and backs of their dun-colored PT suits, although for most of them the morning's exertions had not yet begun as they watched the three men at the center of the ring.

The senior drill's head was not entirely shaven: there was no hair to shave from those wide swaths of his scalp scored by the ropy keloid burn scars. He stood back from the two clumsy, grappling recruits who towered over him, his battle-dress utilities as dry and unstained as if the heat no more dared touch him than either of them would have.

Hallorhan ducked and flailed blindly, evading the grip of the big, grinning farmboy who shifted easily on the balls of his feet and came after him again. He had already outlasted the first two recruits to pair off with the farmboy, who found his bulk and his high-school wrestling well suited to the restricted lethality of the unarmed-combat classes. But Hallorhan had survived so far only by running away, his attempts to apply the throws and locks they had been shown futile.

He watched as the farmboy shuffled forward again, crouched low, arms wide, well balanced and strong. Hallorhan watched him and then jumped forward, placing his feet carefully the way they'd been shown, grabbing the farmboy's sleeve and collar exactly right. Then the farmboy had both hands on Hallorhan's lead arm and he was driving forward and to the outside of Hallorhan's lead foot, using Hallorhan's arm as a lever, overbalancing him, throwing him back—

*Hallorhan twisted, landing on his shoulder instead of flat on his back, avoiding disqualification. He rolled to his knees but the farmboy was on top of him now, one arm around his waist, the other reaching across under his body for Hallorhan's far arm, to pull it through and flip him on his back again like an old mattress—*

*Hallorhan snatched his arm away and twisted wildly, scrabbling to get his feet under him. The farmboy must have been getting overconfident; he lost his grip on Hallorhan's waist and Hallorhan managed to get his feet back under him and retreat again.*

*"Hold it," the senior drill called. The two recruits froze in place as he walked over to Hallorhan.*

*"You're still slowing yourself down," he said. "You're still trying too hard to set everything up."*

*"I'm just trying to get it right," Hallorhan said.*

*The senior drill was nettled. He hadn't been asking for a discussion. "Wrong," he said. "You're thinking about getting it right, and that's fucking you up. Just let it happen. Don't fucking think."*

*He stepped back from between them. "All right. Go." But the big farmboy was moving in already, fleshy hands outstretched and reaching. Hallorhan beat at them and skidded back as the farmboy came on, desperately trying to think of what not fucking thinking felt like.*

*But this time the farmboy had changed his timing. He lunged forward even as Hallorhan struck his hands away. Hallorhan had no time to step aside, no time to retreat farther. He turned and crouched, flinching away, to be honest, his hands flung up to guard his head—*

*He felt an impact against his hip, and then there was a rush of motion along his back and over his head. One of the farmboy's flailing elbows jabbed him painfully in the ear as he tumbled over Hallorhan and landed flat on his ass in the sawdust. He twisted to glare up at Hallorhan and started to rise. Then he fell back, screaming as he put his weight back on the hand he had tried to break his fall with, the fractured wrist already swelling and blackening.*

*The senior drill was there at once, but there was nothing he could do except confirm that the wrist was broken, and then stand there until the medics came into*

the ring and took the farmboy away. Then he turned back
to Hallorhan.

"Like I said," he said, "don't fucking think." He looked
past Hallorhan to the recruits ringing in the pit. "Next."

Hallorhan turned to face his next opponent. The man
rose up out of the wreckage, the flames gleaming on his
Special armor. Blue flame streamed out of his plasma
gauntlet at Hallorhan, seeming to fill the world as it flared
toward him. Hallorhan should have died then, frozen in
astonishment, but the training was working on a level all
its own and his limbs spasmed, his armor flailed to throw
him to one side. It almost wasn't enough: the plasma burst
took him glancingly, across the ribs, and ablative ceramic
that wasn't supposed to burn flared and steamed away as
if it were ice on a stove top. Hallorhan rolled, cursing
indignantly over all the tac channels in sequence, but if
the trooper heard him he gave no sign, stepping forward
and firing again, as Hallorhan rolled away through the
rubble scattered over the street, fire scoring the ground
behind him, gouging the road, melting wreckage already
broken beyond recognition. Hallorhan was on his feet
now, leaping for the safety of a cornerstone, pitting his
evasive skills against the autofire circuits of his voiceless
adversary. Plasma broke against the building like flaming
lava; a line of laser pulses stitched through an abandoned
groundcar behind him. Then he was safe for an instant,
flat on his belly facing back toward the corner. The
trooper came around the corner swiftly, crouched low, and
Hallorhan readied himself to flee again.

"No, dammit!" he shouted. "Stop it!" But even as he
shouted a glowing arrowhead transfixed the whirling trooper and his own gun hand was extending, without the least
volition on his part. The Krupp strobed scarlet across the
street, and now the trooper's armor streamed puffs of
evaporated ablative as the pulses walked their way up his
chest and into his visor. The trooper staggered, firing
wildly, already blind from that portion of the laser energy
that punched through his mirrored faceplate and into
delicate, defenseless retinae. Then he fell, as Hallorhan's
next, unwilled burst struck the damaged visor again and
pierced it completely, visor and face and brain.

"Again, please," the doctor said.

"Why?" Hallorhan demanded tiredly.

"It's necessary, Lieutenant," the unseen voice responded.
"We know what we're doing. Please don't worry about it."

The street flickered back into being around him again,
filling the long, narrow room with storefronts and passersby
and bright daylight, masking completely the off-white
institutional walls.

"Whenever you're ready, Lieutenant."

Hallorhan shrugged and started off up the street, indistinguishable from any of the holographic pedestrians—or
at least as much so as was possible in the floppy hospital
pajamas. The hologram unscrolled ahead of him, granting
the illusion of open space and new sights even if it couldn't
eradicate his awareness of the solid walls that blocked him
in.

Hallorhan walked up the street, the people walked by
him, the traffic flowed past in each direction. The traffic
noise welled up around him in a reassuring murmur,
interlaced with the lulling harmonics crafted to put him off
his guard.

It wasn't a heavy blow, merely a soft impact from the
half-filled sandbag projected through the image of the
man stepping out of the doorway, simulating an average
accidental jostling.

But Hallorhan didn't have time to consider its authentic-
ity until he was face to face with the hologram, staring
back at him placidly through eyes transfixed by his finger-
tips as though by so many spear points. . . .

"Shit," the disembodied doctor-voice said from overhead. Hallorhan had the feeling he wasn't supposed to
have heard that. But he didn't give it any thought.

Moses was surprised to see the lights on in the wardroom. Although day and night were useless terms in the
unchanging now of space flight, most ships kept to the
light and dark cycle of their most recent port of call out of
convenience, to avoid the irritation of changing time cycles
more often than necessary. By Hybreasil time it was deep
night; no one but the watch officer—Moses himself—could
have been expected to be awake.

Hallorhan looked up from his untouched coffee cup as
Moses entered. "Good morning, I think."

"'Day to you," Moses answered. "What are you doing up and about at this hour?"

"I couldn't sleep." Hallorhan shrugged. "A blinding glimpse of the obvious."

"Old war stories again?" Moses unfolded a chair and fetched his own cup.

"Yeah, kind of."

"Care to share them?"

Hallorhan smiled wanly. "No thanks, Captain. They keep me awake, but I've learned from experience that they're guaranteed in writing to put anyone else to sleep."

"As you like, then."

"Thanks for the offer, though."

"Any time," Moses said. "You did a good job on the lift out today."

"Thanks. As good as you could yourself?"

"Ah, piloting's not my line of work, Deacon," Moses said easily.

"You've got your ticket." He shrugged again as Moses looked at him. "I've been reading up. Old habits."

"Yes, well."

"You haven't had it updated in a hell of a long time, though. You should take care of that. Then you wouldn't have to go scraping up oddball pilots like me."

"Oh, I'd still have to scrape up the odd pilot now and again. If I tried to update that ticket they'd pull it faster than the telling of it."

"Why?"

"Why? Because I'm old, Deacon, or getting there. I haven't got the hands or the eyes for piloting anymore, or the nerves to keep them together. Piloting's a young man's game, so get your fill of it before all those little brain cells dry up and make a spectator out of you."

"I guess it all depends which brain cells go first," Deacon said. "So why do you keep the ticket at all?"

"The first law of independent carrying," Moses said. "Waste not, want not. If I turned it in, I'd never get it back now. But as long as I have it, if I ever do have to bring this old bitch down by myself, I've got the paper that says it's legal."

"You don't sound too bitter about it."

"Ah, look, the sort of fellow who'd feel bitter about

getting old is the sort of fellow who'd complain about a grafting revenuer or bad weather."

"I never much cared for weather, myself," Hallorhan said. "Fickle stuff."

"Then you should learn to appreciate its infinite variety. There, you see the advantage of getting old? You can spout twaddle like that and no one laughs at you. Especially when you're their captain and you can order them to wipe that silly grin off their faces, so watch it, Mr. Hallorhan."

"Sorry."

"Mind you, though, it does get to the point sometimes where you're ready to just pitch it all in and sail off into your sunset years on a nice grungy Sunrunner sloop or something."

"Why a Sunrunner?"

"Because it's slow, and useless, and nobody expects anything from you when that's all you've got. You don't go getting mixed up in messes like this one, for instance, because no one thinks they can use you for anything."

"Oh, we'll get through this all right."

"That's not my point, Deacon. I know I'll get through this. I've carried midnight cargoes before. I just resent the need to get through it, or to get involved with it in the first place. I'd just as soon be left alone to make my own living without troubling anyone, and I can't see why they should come looking to mix me into their problems."

"Well, if there's any cure for that, Captain, I don't know what it is."

"Ah, there isn't one, never was. I learned that long enough ago. I'm just getting to the point where I resent more and more being reminded of it. Maybe that's what getting old comes down to, at the end of it."

"That's funny. As I recall, being young felt the same way."

Moses got heavily to his feet. "Yes, well, I don't hear anyone asking our opinion in the matter, so there's no point in worrying about it." He fed his cup back into the dispenser. "Spooky's got the next watch, so you've plenty of time yet, but try and get some sleep before you come back on, won't you?"

"Sure, Captain. See you later."

"I'm not going anywhere."

* * *

Mitsuko's cabin made Moses' look grand. There was no room to pace, even if pacing had been her way. There was room enough to stand or to sit behind the folding desk top; room enough to lie down on the recessed bunk or sit on the open end that served as a chair.

Mitsuko lay on her side, curled up stiffly, as deep into the bunk's recess as she could get. Her eyes were open, but she wasn't looking at the cream-toned bulkhead across from her.

She couldn't find Eisberg. She could hear Moses on the bridge, and from him she knew that Deacon Hallorhan brooded alone in the wardroom. Luther Orange and Nullman slept; nothing there of note under the black and scarlet roiling of their undervoices as they dreamed.

But of Eisberg there was no sign.

She hadn't expected one. She knew where she had to look. But she had made the safe search, the outer search, first, hoping against hope that she would be spared the inevitable necessity. Mitsuko Tamura looked inward.

She remembered.

Childhood, before knowledge, before pain, before her unwanted gift had flowered. Occasional flashes of the talent gave her brief peeks into the minds of parents, teachers, playmates. The adults called her precocious, bright, dear. She was still too young to understand everything she saw and heard; conscious thought and fuliginous undervoice were one and the same to her, repeated back with a child's innocence that robbed her accidental truthfulness of any threat.

Children her own age avoided her, with that unique child's awareness of the uncommon, the strangeness to be avoided, that was born of the juvenile herd instinct and the first fumbling attempts to adopt the adult world's proffered standards of conformity. Their rejection wounded her, in the deceptively slight way of any childhood injury. But she made up for it, if only in part, with the approval of the adults who did not know enough to fear her. It was, on balance, not an unhappy time for her, and she abandoned her search for Eisberg there. He would fasten on her discontents, seek leverage in her miseries.

Then adolescence, and the first real hurting. The betrayal of her own body, changing, growing, echoing needs and desires she didn't even know she had. And with the ripening of her body, the full weight of her talent came to bear down upon her.

The fleeting transparency of the minds around her had cost her the company of her peers in childhood. Now her maturing vision denied her the approval of the adult world upon whose threshold she was hovering. With her first physical maturity came the first distinction between shaped, expressed thought and the turbulent, animal impulses of the undervoice, the shadow hungers and lusts that twisted and stained everything around her. Her precocious expressions of the thoughts echoing around her brought her uncomfortable reprovals instead of applause; what was cute and amusing coming from the mouth of an innocent, uncomprehending young girl was too disturbing when spoken by a nubile child-woman whose nascent sexuality itself began to respond to the gathered impressions.

Sex was a conundrum with which she utterly failed to cope.

Hers was not a backward community. Its youth were not kept in ignorance of their bodies, of the realities of man and woman and their needs. Mitsuko understood the biology of sex, she understood the intended spirit of it. She understood everything they taught her.

Unfortunately, hers was not a backward community. Her teachers were not content with explaining the basic animal mechanics of intercourse. It was important that the emotional and social elements of sex be made clear as well. So her teachers patiently explained to them all the communion of sex, the ultimate sharing and intimacy of intercourse, the deepening and firming of relationships that were born out of that intimacy.

But they never told her about the undervoice.

Down in the undervoice, communion and intimacy and sharing were dry paper concepts that shredded and blew away in the hot, surging winds of simple lust. Her teachers talked of communion and intimacy and sharing, but she received a different set of impressions entirely whenever they looked at the elfin girl-child with the wide, dark, vulnerable eyes, and the discord was a pain in her mind.

It was a pain that followed her everywhere. To her

horror, mommy and daddy didn't "make love," as the teachers expressed it; mommy and daddy *fucked*, reducing each other to a set of basic gratification impulses in the feculent depths of their minds, down where neither of them would admit it, could admit it, even to themselves. Of course, they didn't *fuck* as often or as well as mommy would háve liked anymore, and that was another discordant note that plucked at the overtensed strings of Mitsuko's awareness.

And it was a pain that utterly ruined her own first sexual explorations. Much later, she would learn that telepathy was not a glorified mental radio, shuttling sterile concepts back and forth. It was instead a unification of perception, a merging of identity. She did not perceive the minds of others; she shared them, became part of their identity as they would have found themselves part of hers, had they had the gift to realize it.

But where she became a part of their identity, she could not avoid the realization that on the base, uncontrolled level of the undervoice, they suppressed hers utterly. No matter what they said, no matter what they consciously thought in most scrupulous adherence to their instruction, or perhaps even in sincere belief, down on the level of the undervoice Mitsuko Tamura was not someone to make love with: she was something to be fucked.

Suppression of identity is murder. . . .

Mitsuko looked into the minds of the callow young boys around her and found no perception of herself there, only clumsy, consuming hunger, voracious in its natural innocence, that denied her at the same time it lusted for her. She recoiled; she could not help it, and the friction between her own needs and her fear of theirs was another source of gnawing tension.

She fought it, once, with a young boy in one of her classes, a shy, awkward, bookish youth whose loneliness she thought mirrored her own. She made it as far as his bed, and she tried, she really did, to take pleasure in his bumbling attempts at foreplay. But her damned gift was still there, and his sensations and urges overwhelmed her, stunned her, threatened to drown her in their self-involvement. She had panicked, fighting him off blindly, fleeing his bed and his house in unthinking terror, followed by his shame and embarrassment and confused fear. He had been convinced it was his fault, which it was—but it wasn't, how could he know; he had actually cried. She had never been able to face him in class again, and wallowed in guilty relief when she graduated and matriculated to a college far from home, sped on her way with the verbal blessings of her parents and the unconscious voicing of their relief at their release from responsibility for this incomprehensible child.

She had been twenty-two and still a virgin when the Institute found her.

The contact had been a simple thing. One minute she was alone at the table in the campus library, seeking privacy behind the stultifying numbness of academic prose. The next, he was there, pale and coolly aloof and smiling the smile she would learn to hate.

"Hello, Mitsuko."

She had stared at him in some confusion. "Do I know you?"

"You can, if you want to."

She bristled at what seemed to be a crude collegiate come-on.

"Thank you, but I think I'll pass—"

And then she *did* know him. Suddenly she saw herself sitting there as though watching herself from across the table—she *was*, she realized. And at the same time there came a wash of approval, of brotherly, slightly superior affection, warm and unthreatening.

And then she realized: she had not reached out for it; it had been *sent* to her.

She stared at Eisberg in mute astonishment—and felt her surprise passed back to her, overlaid with a familiar amusement. Delight rose in her, unbidden, at the simple knowledge of the existence of one like her, who would understand, who would *have* to understand—

"Of course I do," he said simply.

"Who are you?" she had asked, unable to frame any question more probing in her happy confusion. "What do you want?"

"I'm someone who wants to help you, Mitsuko."

"Help me? How?"

"You know how. I want to stop the pain. I can show you how."

"How?" she asked. "What do I have to do? Where do I have to go?"

"We'll tell you." And he was gone, as simply and abruptly as he had appeared.

The cunning of it was monumental in its simplicity. Eisberg's appearance had been an amazing shock to her, a tantalizing, joyful instant whose impact could only grow, whose allure could only increase with absence. The constant, steady, daily struggle against the unthinking impositions of the unknowing masses around her assumed a new poignancy through the simple knowledge that something else, something different, something better could exist. And when Eisberg returned for her, after a week, in the flesh this time, she had gone with him willingly.

At first, her time at the Institute had been a paradise to her. Just the knowledge that she was not alone, that there were people who understood her needs and troubles, had seemed to her to be the doorway to a new life. They had taught her, first, to control her own sendings, something she had never learned out in the world of the psychically deaf, for she had walked among them a happy, uncontrolled outpouring of impressions and sensations unchecked by any discretion. Then they had begun the more difficult task of training her to filter out the impressions she received from others. It was a difficult skill, a slow art to master, but even the slightest progress had been a joy to her, offering a relief she had never dreamed possible. She felt complete, in control of her life for the first time. She felt mature.

It couldn't last. It was the security of ignorance, a fleeting protection at best. Because first they taught her to control her gift. Then they showed her how they used it.

"It's time you started earning your keep," Eisberg told her one morning. He spoke aloud, a courteous convention of the school, a token of respect for privacy.

"What do you mean?" Mitsuko asked.

"Our noble Institute has many sterling virtues," he said. "Unfortunately, economy is not one of them. We have our expenses. We have to generate some kind of income to cover them, and for that, we look to our more promising students."

"Well, of course, whatever I can do," she said quickly. "But won't it interfere with my studies?"

Eisberg smiled. "My dear girl, how to apply your gifts is the next thing you must learn."

It was a new revelation to her, that the ability she had thought a handicap should actually have a use, an application by which she might even benefit.

"What do I have to do?" she asked.

"Let me show you," he answered, and then he was moving easily into her mind, with practised familiarity.

"You must open yourself to the world again," he told her, and sensing her reluctance, "I'll be there. Just let it happen."

Carefully she lowered her new-won barriers, and the roar of humanity was upon her once more. She recoiled, ready to retreat, to wall off again the great cascade of selves, but Eisberg was there, in control, and the flood was muted, controllable by the time it reached her.

"Follow me," he instructed, and she let him guide her out into the maelstrom of mankind.

"Deafening, isn't it?"

"What did you say?"

"Very clever. It's hard to make any sense of it all, isn't it? So difficult to distinguish any one of them from the others in all the babble. But there are differences, if you know how to look for them—and those differences can be quite profitable. Look here, observe this one." In the muted rumble of minds around her, one single tone suddenly became clearer. "Learn this pattern; it will be important to your work."

"What is it?" she asked, savoring the sound/taste/feel of it. There was, she decided, a singularity to it, a clarity, however flawed and intermittent, that did distinguish it from the noise surrounding it.

"Well. For want of a better way of expressing it, that is the flavor of art."

"What?"

"That sensation is linked intimately with creativity, exploration, growth. It's quite distinct."

"Umm." Mitsuko rolled it around inside her head. "It has sort of a . . . kind of a selfish feeling to it, somehow."

"Of course. Creativity is an obsessive phenomenon. It doesn't often leave room for other concerns."

"Oh. Well, what's he creating?"

"Why don't we see?"

He guided her down, to drift gently around the fringes of a stranger's awareness, unnoticed.

"He's working," she declared, surprised.

"So he is. Macroprocessor board assembly, it seems."

"But it's a factory. There's dozens of him—er—them down there. What kind of art is that?"

"Look at what he's doing. Those boards come to him as pieces of useless silicon. They leave him as systems, capable of doing work they could never do but for his influence on them. He makes them something new, and he knows this."

"That's art?"

"My dear little Mitsuko, if art were limited to sonnets and popcart authors, this species would be in even sorrier shape than it is now."

"But how does this profit us?"

"In this case, it doesn't. But now you know what to look for. And that will be your first assignment in your new studies. Find us art."

She felt him withdraw slightly, and she hastily took up the burden of shielding that he let slip. Then she lowered it, tentatively, inexpertly, searching through the wow and rumble of the mental cacophony surrounding them. She moved through the jumble, carefully seeking to match some part of it to the memory of the new sensation Eisberg had shown her. Suddenly she felt a whiff of art and pounced on it eagerly, declaring it to Eisberg.

They hunted on throughout the morning, and Mitsuko discovered strand after strand of artistry woven throughout the mesh of human noise around them.

"I don't understand," she confessed after a time. "This is the flavor of art, that's what you called it, right?"

"That's right."

"Then how come I'm not discovering any artists? I mean, *art* artists? I'm finding bankers, boat builders, bricklayers, and buskers. Where are the painters, the popcart authors, the sculptors? Aren't there any artists interested in art?"

"Very few, fortunately. Otherwise we'd be hip-deep in the stuff."

"Then what are they all doing?"

"Making a living, in the main—just like the bankers, boat builders, bricklayers, and buskers. Don't confuse a certain facility of expression with artistry. There's a difference, perhaps only of intention or perception, but a difference."

"Oh. And what if they're sure they're artists, but I can't find the flavor?"

"Then they're most likely bad artists. There's nothing that prevents such a thing."

"Whatever you say. Hello."

"Another one?"

"Looks like it."

"Where?"

"Here." Mitsuko guided him onto the thread, flattered that he let her. "Another artistic assembly-line worker."

"Yes . . . but this one we can use."

"What do you mean?"

"Look at that system he's working on, and listen to him."

"What about it?"

"It's new. It hasn't even been announced yet."

"So what?"

"So now we turn this over to our experts. If this system is at all promising, and we invest in this firm quickly enough, we stand to make a handsome profit."

"Oh?"

"What's the matter?"

"Well . . . is that right?"

"Right? Whatever do you mean, right?"

"It doesn't seem right, somehow. It seems as if we're taking advantage."

"How? You have two good eyes, don't you?"

"Yes . . . ?"

"Well, if you were to go walking down the street and those two good eyes saw money lying in the gutter, would you feel you had taken advantage of whoever left it there? Of course you wouldn't."

Mitsuko worried the idea around. "It isn't the same. These people haven't *lost* anything. It's still theirs, and we're just coming along and taking it."

"We don't take anything. We don't deny them anything. They are simply there, and we're using the opportunity to benefit ourselves along with them."

"But we haven't done anything to deserve it."

"Dear little Mitsuko. No one ever deserves anything. That's a concept dreamt up by people who couldn't fend for themselves."

"But—"

"Trust us in this. We know. And you'll learn."

She learned. She spent the following weeks assiduously braving the unsuspecting masses as if she were some psychic rag-and-bone man rummaging through a midden heap in search of a stray garnet. Every once in a while she would come upon a bright awareness with the flavor of art to it and eagerly summon Eisberg, who, every rarer once in a while—to hear him tell it—deigned to pass her discovery on to the people prepared to exploit it for the Institute.

It was almost a month before she thought to turn her new skills upon the Institute itself.

It was not a planned action. It happened at two o'clock in the morning, when she could not sleep and was bored. In truth, it was not an action she would ever have taken had she actually thought about it. There was a sense of community to her life at the Institute that she had never known before, an incomparable sense of belonging. She would never deliberately have put that at risk. But it was late, she was bored, and she acted on impulse.

She reached out cautiously, into the nighttime silence of the Institute, mindful of their unspoken conventions of privacy. Off in the somnolent quiet of the Institute, she became aware of others awake and communicating. With all the care she was capable of, she moved in on the interchange, delicately seeking to interject herself just far enough to follow the dialogue. She had almost abandoned the effort when she realized that she was eavesdropping on Eisberg and one of the other senior instructors. But they did not seem to have noticed her, and her curiosity was strong. She eased in, to better discern the object of their interest.

It was herself, and what they were doing filled her with loathing.

She was naked in their minds, and Eisberg was doing things to her, like the things the boys had tried to do in school, that she hated. But in Eisberg's mind she was *letting* him, in his mind she *liked* it, and liked the fact that it was *him* doing it.

Her horror made her careless. She suddenly sensed that Eisberg was aware of her presence. She tried to withdraw, to flee, but he reached out and held her in the link, effortlessly.

"Let go of me!" she protested, struggling to break the link. But this was a level of skill unfamiliar to her; she was not even certain how she was being held in the link against her will. "Damn you, stop it!"

"I can't imagine what you're so indignant about," he said coldly. "After all, you're the one trying to sneak around in other people's minds." There was something different about him here, she saw. He had always affected an air of amused superiority around her before, an attitude she had never questioned. He was more experienced than she was in the use of his talent; he did know more; he had abilities she knew she couldn't match. But now she saw that he enjoyed this power over her, in a way that frightened her inexpressibly.

The image of her was still clear in his mind.

"How could you do that?" she cried. "Stop it!"

"What I do in the privacy of my own intellect is my own affair," he answered. "It would never have troubled you had you not forgotten your most basic courtesies. Besides, I cannot believe this is something you haven't seen before— but it's true, you haven't," he abruptly corrected himself, as nearly surprised as she had ever seen him. "I don't believe it." The fact of it seemed to amuse him even more.

"That's none of your business!"

"On the contrary. I am responsible for your education. I would be derelict in my office were I to neglect this most important aspect."

"You leave me the hell alone!" But there was nothing

she could do as she felt him reach down deep into her mind.

He *touched* her then, in a way that made her flush, warmed and outraged all at once. Alone in her room, she writhed to the touch of immaterial hands as he moved through her soul like a serpent sliding through silk, arousing in her sensations she had rejected years before but that overwhelmed her now, with no one to oppose. He wasn't imposing those sensations, she realized, helpless in the knowledge, he was releasing them, dredging them up out of her. She could not oppose them because they were hers to begin with—and yet they were not hers, because she had denied them and would not have awakened them voluntarily.

She was never certain afterward when he joined her corporeally, when intangible sensation had fused with a physical coupling she could not help accepting. Even the actual, physical pain, when it came, was half lost in a haze of forced arousal. The next inarguably real feeling she was aware of was the warm scarlet wetness underneath her where she was huddled on the bed, glaring up at him.

"You bastard," she sobbed. "You goddamned bastard." His mind was closed to her now; he wanted no part of her anger or hurt. He ignored her curses; he was *grinning*, she saw. He finished pulling on his shirt and left her without a word.

She left the Institute the next day.

Six years later, she still could not control the hot rush of impotent rage the memory brought on. It overwhelmed her, blurred even the recollection of the outrage—no. The memory was blurred, she realized, but not from anger.

"Get the hell out of there," she demanded, white-lipped. Suddenly she was back in the library, facing Eisberg once more.

"I should have known to look for you there," she said. "You'd never miss a chance to cop a think, would you?"

"Not at all," he answered smoothly. "I simply couldn't think of a more graphic reminder of how much you have to learn. I trust the point was not lost?"

"The point—? That was *rape*, you bastard! What the hell was that supposed to *teach* me?"

"How could it have been rape? I forced nothing on you. Every urge you responded to was your own, admit that."

"Except the urge to let myself respond. That wasn't me, that was you."

"I imposed nothing. I merely freed what was already there."

"That's right. You freed me. You gave me every freedom except the choice about what I wanted to free."

"But you see, choice is the prerogative of those with the ability to use it."

Her anger had risen to the point where it was self-defeating, so vast and intense that it precluded thought or action. "God help you if I ever meet you again."

"Well, then, it's fortunate for me that you never shall. And it's fortunate for you, because you haven't the skill to face me. You've learned a little since you left us. There's almost no avoiding that. But you don't know nearly enough. You know a couple of monkey tricks, but nothing of the fundamentals of our gift." He paused, for effect. "But if you'd like to learn . . ."

"If I don't?"

"If you don't, it will be a shame, because there's no way you can avoid confronting James Emerson White now. And if you don't accept what I can teach you, he will most assuredly kill you."

"Just as you want it."

"As I said, choice is the prerogative of those who can use it." He forestalled her next protest with a raised hand. "We're both wasting our time. Consider this your first lesson."

The universe went dark around her. In spite of herself, she let out a sharp yelp of alarm—or would have. There was no sound, no change in the impenetrable psychic darkness that enfolded her. Mitsuko had no perception of the medium through which she drifted; to her surprise, she discovered she had no perception of a "she" to drift through the medium with. Her every sense was muffled, shut away. She was a nonentity drifting through nothingness, denied even the event of dissolution for want of a substance to dissolve.

"Each of us suffers from the obligation to recreate our existence from day to day," Eisberg's voice pierced the blackness, coming from every direction and no direction at once.

*Wonderful*, Mitsuko thought bitterly, for want of any other action within her power, *an existential rapist*.

"But what has never been made clear is that each of us is possessed of precisely the ability to do just that. Remember Heisenberg. You shape yourself by your perception of yourself. No other input is valid."

*Listen to yourself, rapist.*

"Perhaps if you had had the patience to master your gift, you would not be vulnerable to such an assault."

*Fuck you.*

"You did." Her anger flared anew, fire with no vessel to contain it. "Yes. Good. You retain enough sense of self to respond to a goad. Take that anger. It is real. Build on it. Bring Mitsuko Tamura back. No one else can find her."

Mitsuko sought through the darkness around her. The anger was a white-hot solidity at the center of her being—but all else was nothing. She extended herself into the dark, endlessly, it seemed. And the farther she went, the farther she expanded from that core of rage, which began to pale and cool with distance. As it faded the fear began to grow within her (or was it within?), as she felt herself drawn thin and threadbare in the infinite night.

*Dammit, help.*

"No. If you can't help yourself, I cannot use you. You're worthless to me."

The anger was fanned up bright again. She clung to it this time, drawing on it even as she fed it, stoked it with more rage against Eisberg and his callous arrogance, building on it.

Suddenly he was there, lit starkly by the fire of her outrage. She willed the flames to even greater brilliance, their glare stripping away more and more of the enshrouding blackness between herself and that hated face—

—and then she was back, trembling and rigid in the middle of the plush acrebeast carpet, while Eisberg studied her with what might almost have been approval.

"Very good," he said. "For a start."

# CHAPTER 7

Spearhead of a javelin of light, the *Wild Goose* pressed its volitant challenge to the distant, impassive stars with a speed no world could check any longer. But the view through the small porthole in the wardroom was static, fixed: the ancient suns the old ship sought spanned too vast a horizon to suffer any change of perspective lightly.

Luther Orange studied their remote brilliance with no little sadness. The porthole was not a great deal larger than the viewports of a ship's flight deck, showing nothing they would not—but Luther Orange was fully aware of the difference between them. The wardroom porthole was a convenience for passengers. It displayed scenes the ship hurtled past. The viewports of the flight deck looked ahead. They opened out, however inadequately, on the vessel's goal. The people who used the wardroom porthole were being borne passively on their way. The flight deck viewports were for crew. They had purpose, they were for people in control of their traveling.

It wasn't so long ago that Luther Orange had been one of them, that he had mastered ships and gone his own way. That he had been, for a time, free.

*We both know the lie of that,* the foreign thought came, unbidden. *From what were you free, Captain? You had a crew to feed and pay and care for. You had clients to satisfy; you carried their wares how and where and when they demanded, in exchange for barely enough money to begin the cycle all over again, if you were lucky. And you had a bank to satisfy, that held your notes—of course, you didn't satisfy them, did you? Or you'd still be master of*

87

*the Boyne.... For a free man, Captain, you seemed most straitly bound.*

"All right, dammit."

*Of course, if that sort of liberty appeals to you, it could be yours again.*

"It could, could it? How?"

*I would let you have it.*

"Just like that, hey?"

*If it suited me.*

"Oh, spare me. What suits you is getting your way, nothing else. I've learned that much, at least."

*You surprise me, Captain. There have been times when I would have doubted you had benefited from our association even to that extent. You're correct, of course. But you want a ship, and I believe I want you to have one—if you'd like.*

"If I'd like," Luther Orange said sarcastically. "Hell, who would I have to kill?"

*Probably no one. We have the redoubtable Mr. Nullman for that.*

"What, this one?"

*You think well of it.*

"It's got a captain," Luther Orange said.

*And the Bethe trigger had an owner. We both know the importance of that. Don't confuse your squeamishness with pragmatic caution, Captain. We both know you too well for that. This ship has a captain, as you say—and if he gets his way, he'll turn the trigger back to the authorities the minute we reach Avalon. I don't have to tolerate being balked so clumsily, and I won't. I appreciate the convenience of having a ship to hand. I don't appreciate having to depend on someone else for its availability. Much better to have a ship of my own, I think. You would captain it, and I would be*—there was that chuckle Luther hated—*well, owner aboard, as it were.*

"You can't just take a starship," Luther Orange protested. "It's too obvious, too public. There's registration, title, public records."

*I won't have to take it. I want him to give it to me. And, soon enough, so will he.*

Moses stepped out into the narrow corridor, stretching the stiffness of sleep out of his back and neck. It always seemed to take a little longer now. He made his way toward the bridge the long way around, checking the sealed hatches to engine room and holds. The locks were in place, seemingly untampered with.

The door to the wardroom was open as he passed. Hallorhan looked up from his table as Moses paused at the door.

"Good morning, Captain."

"I thought I told you to get some sleep."

"I did. Just yesterday."

"Oh." Moses conceded the argument. "Well, you might consider making a habit of it."

"No, no thanks, Captain. Habits can get you into a rut."

"Falling asleep at your board could dig us one."

"I never have yet. It's all right, Captain, I get all the sleep I can use."

"Do you, then?" But it was an automatic attempt at the last word, nothing more.

Light assaulted his eyes as he entered the flight deck: primary illumination bars, backup lanterns, board lamps all turned up full and glaring. The flight deck was full of light, overflowing. There was no slightest hint of shadow, no smallest trace of softening darkness.

"Spooky? Spooky, what the hell are you doing?" He ducked and twisted to face the tech pit behind him and recoiled, his face inches from hers.

He had found the one place on the flight deck the light didn't reach. Her eyes were bottomless ebony pits, into which the fierce light fell and vanished without effect. It was if they opened a door onto midnight in the middle of a desert afternoon. She stared at him with a puzzled, faintly hostile expression somehow more disquieting than her usual skittishness.

"Are you all right?" Moses asked. "What's with all the lights?"

"I wanted them on," she stated, challenging him to dispute it. "It was too dark in here."

"Since when has that bothered you?"

"Since it has, Moses."

"You're sure—"

"I'm all right." She made a visible effort to take the edge

off her attitude. "It's all right, Captain. I just wanted it a little brighter in here, that's all."

"Well, you certainly got that," he said dubiously. He had the sudden feeling that there was a great deal, too much, going on aboard his ship that he wasn't aware of—and couldn't control. But he had no idea what he could do about it, which was as disquieting as the unease itself.

"I relieve you," Moses said at last, seeking refuge in routine. "What's your status?"

"Boards all nominal," she said, forcing casualness. "Or as nominal as they're ever going to get around here."

"Right, I confirm that," he said formally, sliding into his own seat and calling up displays in front of him.

"How much longer before we're ready to jump the curve?" Mitsuko asked. Moses reached out and dialed down his board lamp. It didn't make much difference.

"I was thinking of giving it another week to build up a really good referent vector," he said. "I'm not so sure now. I'm thinking more and more—there's nothing I want worse than just to get there and get that horror out of my holds and the hell off my ship. I think I'd rather play around with insystem vector shifts and make up the time we lose that way than spend one day more in this lash-up than I have to. Because I'm scared, Spooky, and I'm not sure why, and that frightens me even more. I can't turn around without finding my pilot lurking in the corner at all hours of the day and night, I've got an illegal bomb on board that at least one man has died for already, I've got two passengers forced on me who I know are mixed up with that, and now you're acting even weirder than usual. I want shut of this, and the sooner the better."

"So how long?"

Moses punched up the elapsed time and distance display. "Maybe three days."

"I think you're right," Mitsuko said. "I think we should get this over with quickly."

"You're agreeing with me? Now I'm really worried. You've never done that before."

"I'm sorry," she said. "I don't mean to be a bother."

"You said that too seriously."

"I'm sor—did I? I must be more tired than I thought. Maybe I'd better just get to bed."

"Maybe. All right, I have the deck."

"The deck is yours."

The hatch slid shut behind her and Moses bent to his board and began dialing down the lights, lowering their intensity until they were no brighter than the telltales before him, and the stars were visible again through the slitted ports.

The hatch was cold against her back as Mitsuko sagged back against it. Moses hadn't been lying. His fear had been a tangible thing, a tremulous wave of uncertainty jarringly out of character for the old captain. And she had to accept that she was part of the cause of that fear, that his tolerance for what he perceived as her eccentric ways was an added strain that he was now less able to afford—

"Sentimental rubbish," Eisberg opined.

"Who asked you?"

"Your captain's nervous twinges are not your concern. His weakness is his problem."

"It's my problem when I contribute to them."

"Not at all. What right has he to expect you to distort yourself to his expectations? And why should you tolerate it when you have the ability to live to your own satisfaction?"

"Because I have no more right to inflict my peculiarities on him than he has to inflict his on me."

"To talk of rights is irrelevant. You have the ability to arrange things to your desire, and choice is the province—"

"—of those with the ability to use it. The hell with that. The hell with you."

"You're a slower student than I'd hoped you'd be," Eisberg sighed, and the blackness was back again.

Mitsuko didn't have to summon the anger this time. It was already there; it had never left her since the humiliation of her first lesson. She rode it outward, tearing the dark asunder like so many veils of black muslin.

But she could not find Eisberg.

The darkness parted before her without effort, but there was no sign of her scornful manipulator. With no other choice she rushed onward, moving, if only to focus on the knowledge of her motion, to give her some sort of referent in the oblivion that enfolded her.

Then she heard it. The "voice," Eisberg's, so faint and seemingly distant as to be all but unintelligible—but there. It seemed to be coming from everywhere at once, like the sound of breakers in an ocean fog. Mitsuko slowed, hesitated, then picked a direction, almost randomly, and set out in pursuit of that far-off mocking.

Almost at once, she was back in the familiar, hated study.

"Well, that's something, at least," Eisberg admitted. "I frankly didn't think you had the sensitivity to find your way back from so far in."

"Too bad for you that I did. Then you could have had the fun of dealing with White yourself."

"No, actually, I couldn't have. You overrate me, you know. I'm merely a construct, remember. A nodality is really a very limited tool; it's quite annoying sometimes. I can't even find James Emerson White without you."

"The hell you can't. You pointed him out to me."

"Not at all. I identified him for you after you discovered him yourself. You provided the perception. I have no awareness beyond that you provide, sorry as that is. So please don't count on me to do your job for you. That would be a fatal miscalculation."

"I might almost accept that. If I go, you go with me."

"But that doesn't alarm me. If you die, 'I' lose a tool, nothing more. But if you die, you're, well, you're dead." He smiled and spread his hands. "It hardly seems an equitable exchange to me. But then, I never have understood your values."

"You've never understood values, period. Let me out of here."

"The lesson isn't finished."

"Oh, yes, it is."

"That isn't your choice."

"No?" It was Mitsuko's turn to smile. "Then let's just see what I've learned."

She turned away from Eisberg and reached out, seeking for the blackness that had borne her there—

—and the corridor was solid around her again, the only

anomaly Eisberg's presence. To her surprise, he actually looked disconcerted.

"Don't ever do that again," he warned her.

"What's to stop me?"

"You don't understand. The dark isn't someplace you go. It's someplace you send people."

"What's the difference?"

"The difference is that without an external point of reference, you'd never find your way back."

"Oh, that would put you off, wouldn't it? Just you and me down there for the rest of whatever. You'd never accomplish your mission that way, would you? Even for a mere tool, that must be an alarming prospect."

"That's an insane price to pay for such petty revenge."

"But it's a choice, isn't it, where I didn't have a choice before. And choice is the prerogative of those with the ability to use it."

"You don't know what you'd be choosing."

"Then don't push me to choose it. *Leave me the hell alone.*"

"Leave you alone for what?" Hallorhan asked.

She had spoken aloud, Mitsuko realized, and loudly. The lanky pilot was standing in the doorway of the wardroom, staring at her.

"It was nothing," she said quickly, hoping he'd mistake her anger for embarrassment. "You know how captains can get sometimes."

"Yes, I do. Of course, I never stood around shouting at them through bulkheads."

"That's the best way," she said. "What they can't hear, can't hurt me."

He was still staring. She had no way of knowing whether he accepted the lie or not. Her perception of him ended at his face, at those shuttered, noncommittal eyes. The silence in the back of her mind was uncanny. It was as if he rested at the center of a pool of clear, heavy oil that damped down and swallowed all disturbances around him.

She watched him come to a decision. "I suppose that's one way of handling it," he said, and didn't press the matter further.

"It works, sometimes. Usually."

"Glad to hear it. You want anything to eat?"

"Not right now, thank you. I think I'll just go back to my cabin."

"Up to you." He stepped back into the hatchway to let her pass. "Mitsuko."

"What?"

"I'll give you a call when I'm done in here."

"Oh. Thank you." It was an unexpected civility.

She moved on down the corridor to her own cabin, just forward of the engine-room hatchway. It was a cabin in name only, a makeshift utilization of waste space by the addition of an inset berth and lockers. But it was conveniently adjacent to her post, which saved her unnecessary trips into the more populous regions of the ship, and it had a lock on the door.

She threw herself into the berth, seeking the false concealment of the claustrophobically close bulkheads hemming her in. The cabin lights, dialed up full, glared painfully—but she would not face the darkness again.

She turned her back to the cabin and shut her eyes. But she could not sleep in such appalling din. Moses sat alone on the bridge with his fear, images of the crated trigger in the hold merging with Luther Orange's avuncular face grown monstrous and leering over a scene of body bags flickering scarlet under police strobes. Luther Orange slept, the turbulent murk of his somnolent undervoice overlaid with White's malignant presence. Nullman slept as well, his dreams bright with the memory of murder. It was a cacophony of consciousness that permitted her no rest. . . .

Hallorhan looked up as Mitsuko walked into the wardroom. He looked as if he were about to speak, but something in her expression silenced him. She sat down heavily in a corner, not bothering to unlatch a seat, crossed her arms over her knees, and stared.

Hallorhan couldn't let the silence last.

"Can I get you something?" he asked.

"No. Thank you." She barely lifted her chin from her arms far enough to speak. Her gaze never left his face.

"Oh." He made a project out of draining his own cup, unavoidably conscious of her scrutiny.

Mitsuko reached out for the silence he radiated, wrapping it around her awareness, focusing on it to the exclusion of all the mental clutter surrounding her. It was no barrier in itself, but it provided something she could concentrate on, some point toward which she could direct herself, away from all else. But she didn't have to face the fierce, involved stare she fixed on Deacon Hallorhan—and plainly he didn't wish to, either.

"I thought you were going back to your cabin," he said.

"Too noisy," she said, shortly.

"Whatever you say." Hallorhan rose, folding back his chair. "I'll just leave you to your business—" He started for the hatch, taking his aura of silence with him. The possibility of its absence cut her like a knife.

"Why did you leave the service?" she asked quickly, to forestall him. Too quickly: it came out like an accusation. She saw him hesitate, then choose to answer.

"I didn't leave, as such," he said. "I was sort of 'progressively disaffiliated,' to hear them tell it."

"You were thrown out."

"I was discharged. Without prejudice. Honorably, even."

"But they discharged you." It was impossible to hold a conversation this way. She was forced to depend on his words, and they were shadows, shifting and without substance. But if she let him leave, his silence would leave with him. . . .

"I became what they called 'contextually redundant.'"

"So you were pensioned off."

"Can I ask you why you're so interested in this?"

"You're aboard my ship. I have to live with you."

"That's what the captain said on Hybreasil. But even he didn't ask so many questions."

"Moses needed a pilot. He would have signed you on if you'd showed up at the ship with three cops and four outraged fathers right behind you."

"That's pretty much what he said." Hallorhan looked at her, puzzled. No matter what he said, he had the feeling she was listening for something beyond it, some level of meaning he did not know how to evoke.

"So you weren't the perfect soldier, and they paid you off."

"Actually, it was pretty much the other way around. I was a little too good for their liking."

"They let you go for that?"

"Well, it was the agreement we had. I'd stop acting like a human tank and they'd let me out of the soft room."

"You were a psychiatric release?"

"Hell, no. No one's going to give a psychiatric a pilot's ticket. I hold an honorable discharge. I've even got an inactive reserve commission, although I don't expect them to call me up anytime soon."

"They give commissions to the people in the soft rooms?"

"I used to suspect as much, sometimes. Actually, what it was, they felt a little embarrassed about putting me there, so they cobbled me back together and gave me the rank as a going-away present. Also, the reserve commission keeps me accountable under military law in case I ever annoy them—but we're not supposed to think of it like that. Does this bother you?"

"Who, me? You're talking to Spooky Tamura, the little girl who likes to hide in corners, remember? We crazies can't go around judging each other. We'd never have time for anything else."

"That's true enough. But this crazy has got to go now. The captain's been on me to get some sleep, and he might be right."

"I'll walk with you." His look changed. For a moment, she regretted that she couldn't hear him.

"All right."

He was silent as they walked down the narrow corridor, separated by an immeasurable gulf of inches.

They came to his cabin door.

"Well, this is where I say good night, or good morning, or whatever," he said.

"I'll see you, then," Mitsuko said, not moving.

"Almost certainly," he agreed. "Unless you'd rather come in now."

Mitsuko hadn't been surprised like that since school. Hallorhan's unique silence put her completely off-guard.

"No," she said, visibly flustered. She might even have retreated a step, she didn't remember. "No, I have some things to do yet. I can't."

"All right," Hallorhan said. "Then I'll see you later."

The cabin hatch slid shut behind him, locking Mitsuko out in the ship's corridor, alone again with all the tormenting voices.

* * *

Moses leaned back in his chair and watched the systems-update scan scroll up across his terminal. The words and numbers climbed past, giving an impression of order and comprehensibility belied by Moses' knowledge of the aged metal they described. He laid his head back against the headrest, to look out the viewport before him upon the chill, unchanging stars.

The illusion of comfort they offered him was lost. Usually it was possible for Moses to look out on the limitless distances before him and imagine that he could put those distances between himself and his troubles, that there was always somewhere better, or at least untried, that he could go for a fresh start. He could always flee a little deeper into the outer spheres of Confederate space, away from the bigger companies with their newer ships and younger captains, away from the groundside merchants who knew Moses Callahan and the way he did business too well for profit.

But now he could not run, for his troubles lay crated in his holds and traveling in his cabins, binding him to a destination he knew to be a point of violent climax for all the schemes that enmeshed him.

He felt angry. He felt helpless. He felt old.

He had been joking when he discussed retiring with Deacon Hallorhan. For all the appeal he claimed for a life of leisure, the prospect of whole years ahead of him stripped of responsibility or purpose dismayed him. The *Wild Goose* was his world, its maintenance and prosperity his grail—or so he chose to think. The trouble with that was the universe's perverse insistence on intruding into his tight little world with its greeds and factions and world-destroying bombs. He knew himself too well. The possibility that something as weak and insignificant as Moses Callahan, poor merchant captain and old man, could be the only thing standing between millions of people and searing death was an absurdity, a declaration that the ordered fabric of the universe was unraveling at a pace impossible to deal with. In a universe so chaotic, there was no place safe to run. God only knew what was going on where he couldn't see it.

Against such madness, Moses' one spark of virtue seemed a quixotic, ludicrous affectation. It was almost presumptuous of him to assume he had any right to make himself responsible for the welfare of so many strangers, and farcical to think he could pull it off.

And if that train of thought was not entirely his own, he never realized it.

*"Captain Callahan?"*

The summons from the intercom roused him from his bleak reverie.

"Yes, Captain Orange?"

*"Permission to visit the bridge, sir?"*

Moses' first reaction was refusal. Luther Orange was a threat, the man had admitted as much. But the security scanners showed him to be unarmed and alone, and just at that moment Moses Callahan wasn't too sure there was anything to be on guard *for*, anyway. He cleared the locks on the flight deck hatch.

"Come ahead."

The illumination from the overhead light bars dimmed as Luther Orange interposed his bulk between them and the captain's station, crouched uncomfortably on the entry deck.

"Just like I remembered it," he said, grinning, chins tucked into his chest to clear the bulkhead.

"Take a seat," Moses offered, waving a hand at the pilot's station.

Luther Orange eased himself ponderously down into Hallorhan's chair. He reached up and handed Moses a foaming beaker over the intervening consoles, and laughed at Moses' dubious expression.

"Isn't that being a bit melodramatic, Captain?"

"I wouldn't know," Moses said. "The mundane side of life hasn't been much in evidence lately, you have to admit."

"Perhaps not," Luther Orange answered, "but it would still be a sloppy way to do business. I can hardly fly a ship by myself. Besides, I've no need to do you harm, Captain."

"Don't you, now? We both know what I'm carrying, don't we?"

"Certainly."

"And you must know I'm not likely to just turn it over peacefully."

"But I don't know that, Captain."

"Then you're not as smart as I thought you were," Moses said, nettled by Luther Orange's easy assumption of his venality.

"Oh, I know you don't mean to right now," he said easily. "That's why I'm here."

"To persuade me? That will take some doing."

"Then I'd best get started. What are your objections to letting us have the trigger, Captain? What will it cost you? You've been paid, no one can prove you had any knowledge of the true nature of your cargo, and I hardly think you're going to remain on Avalon long enough to be concerned about its possible use, are you?"

"All true enough," Moses said. "But you leave out one detail."

"Which is?"

"I'm no gunrunner. I haven't the stomach for turning over something like the trigger to the League."

"To who? The League? Oh, no, Captain." Luther Orange's amusement seemed genuine. "We want nothing to do with those vest-pocket empire builders, any more than you do. No, the party I represent has good and sufficient uses of his own for a Bethe trigger, to be sure, but conquering the stars for mankind's eternal glory isn't one of them. Besides, one trigger would be a bit scanty for the job, wouldn't it?"

"I'm not sure there can be a good and sufficient use of a Bethe trigger," Moses said. "And I'm less sure there's a reason for me to give one up to someone who thinks there is."

"Axyll Jakubowski had a reason that suited you."

"Axyll Jakubowski was insane. If I hadn't been broke I'd never have listened to him. And now Axyll Jakubowski's dead, because someone else wanted that trigger as badly as he did."

"That wasn't our doing." The lie came smoothly to Luther Orange's lips. White would have been proud of him.

"So you say. I've no way of proving that, one way or the other. And I'll be damned if I'll give it up and take a chance on my being wrong."

"I don't see why that should concern you, Captain. I can assure you that we have no intention of actually using the weapon. And in any case, you won't be around to have to worry about it. This entire region is going corporate-line. You'll never be back this way again."

"Ah, well, as I said, I haven't the stomach for gunrunning. You see, I'd know what I'd done, and I'm not prepared to live with that memory, or the knowledge of what I'd have made possible. And I don't think there's anything you can say to convince me otherwise."

"That's unfortunate."

"Yes, it is, and perhaps we'd best just let the matter lie there," Moses suggested. "Otherwise you're going to have to start making threats, and I'm really not in the mood for that."

"As you wish." Luther Orange turned to look out the viewport before him. Presently he relaxed, falling under the spell of the swath of starscape it presented.

"This does bring back memories," he said.

"Yes," Moses answered. "You said you'd gotten your start in Wander Birds. Did you ever captain one?"

"Oh, God, no. I was a *child* then, Captain. No, I apprenticed and won my third officer's ticket aboard the old *Kestrel*. I won my first command with the *Boyne*. That was a good nineteen years ago, easy."

"The *Boyne*—she'd be a Mississippi-class carrier?"

Luther Orange nodded. "Ten-kilotons, orbit-to-orbit container hauling. You ever serve aboard a Mississippi, Captain?"

"Can't say as I did. I came up out of the intrasystem classes, picked up my shift ticket later."

"They were great ships. Wonderful bridge. You could stand up to that one great port and dare the stars to try their stuff against you; it was like you stood at the edge of the world, it really was. And you could have lashed four of these ladies to her and still had room for more. No offense, Captain."

"None taken. I took my measure a long time ago. Why'd you give it up, then?"

"It wasn't exactly my idea at the time. Like I said, the Mississippis were container haulers, very advanced designs of the type, too. Trouble with that is, you need a lot of support for a container system. You need a colony with orbital docking and the wealth to justify a highside port. And you know how far in you have to go to find that."

"Not as far as you used to."

"Well, no, true, but the thing is, the farther in from the border you come, the more you start playing against the corporate lines." He paused to sip at his beaker. "Well, I could take care of myself in that crowd, at least as long as the lines were only running ten- and twenty-kiloton designs themselves. I was marginal, but I stayed competitive.

"Of course, you know what happened then, don't you? The big liners, the fifties, started coming out from the core. There just wasn't any competing with them. You'd slash your profit to the bone and they'd still beat you out, riding on their capital and outcarrying you five to one.

"So I did what everyone else does: I started moving out, ahead of the lines. Only trouble with that is, there's just so far an orbit-to-orbit carrier can go. You can do business anyplace you can get this old lady down on the ground, but you can only go so far out before you run out of highside ports."

"What happened?"

"Last I heard, the bank had stripped her of her shift gear and was using her as an orbital hulk until they get their *real* highside port finished."

"Damn."

"Yeah. Well, I hopped from system to system through the Missions, but it's not too easy to get another command when you lost your last one to the bank. Collisions, melt-downs, shift errors, they're all just one of those things, but losing money? That's unforgivable.

"So I wasted months, years, running around before it sank in—I wasn't ever going to get another command. Never. That's when I learned my next lesson, Captain. If you have to play with money, play with someone else's. The odds are better and the responsibilities aren't yours."

"And that's what you're doing now, is it?"

"*You* could do it, Moses. Come in with us. Imagine what a going concern you could make of this old girl with some decent capital behind her. No more scrimping and saving, scraping by on old systems and tired luck, no more being shafted by every petty shipper down below."

"And no more my ship, either," Moses said quietly. "I don't think I could function as an employee."

"You're an employee now, Captain," Luther Orange said. "Do you think they give a damn for your independence down in the Warrens? Not unless they can use it, they don't. You need their money a lot more than they need your ship."

"But I can still choose whose money I take."

"The hell you can, or you wouldn't be here now."

"That's true enough," Moses said bleakly. "But what would I gain otherwise? I'd just be trading several masters I could leave for one master I was stuck with, wouldn't I? All I'd be giving up would be my responsibility for my crew, my ship, and myself, and I'd rather not do that, thank you very much. It goes with the braid."

"That's so damned naive."

"Quite likely. But I'll bet you'd have said it once yourself, when you stood your own watches."

Luther Orange gave the only answer to that he could, rising to his feet and climbing up out of the pilot's station in one long step. He turned to look down at Moses from the access deck.

"Have it your own way, then, Captain. But this world wasn't put here for you to play your little games in."

"Captain Orange," Moses said, with a certainty that surprised even himself, "I've no time for a world that calls my life a game. Now, get off my flight deck."

He swung back to his board, and for a time he actually felt like someone he wouldn't mind knowing again. But then the fear came creeping back, soft moth-wing flutters of despair and doubt seeking the bright flame of his vigor once again. . . .

*Captain.*

*Captain.*

*Damn you, don't you* dare *ignore me!*

The force of the thought brought Luther Orange up short along the corridor. He stood, staring blindly, swaying like a bull wearied by the persistent provocations and barbs of the picadors.

*I'm disappointed, Captain. You didn't do a very good job of persuading him.*

"No," Luther Orange said, "you're right. I didn't. Because, goddamn him, he's right. You haven't got anything to offer him."

*I can offer him exactly what I offered you, Captain.*

*Freedom. From fear of being used. From fear of losing his ship. From fear of failing himself.*

"He doesn't want it, just like I wouldn't have, once."

*But you want it now. And he* will *want it. I will ensure it. I'll give him all the chances he needs to surrender, as you surrendered. Because that's all that's needed to never fear again. Make my will yours, because I fear nothing. And then you won't need to fear, either.*

"And what if he chooses to be afraid?"

*He won't. They never do.*

# CHAPTER 8

*To his amazement, he had actually reached his target.*

*The building bulked large before him, unmistakable as much for the square, utilitarian lines of its construction as for the clustered antennae and radomes that swept the sky above the embattled city. All around the horizon, bright, bar-straight lines of energy reached up into the sky, interlaced with the bright coals of ascending missiles. Far overhead, deep within the sky, Hallorhan might have seen the birth of new, impossible suns, visible in daylight for the whole of their brief life. But he did not look. All his attention was riveted on the building ahead of him, and on the squads and platoons and swarms of Mishiman troops moving to bar him from it. He could not recall the last time he had seen another Special fighting his way toward their goal, but the Mishimans produced troops in an endless flood that threatened to swamp him by sheer numbers.*

*The laser in his right hand was still on autofire, had forever been on autofire, cutting down one Mishiman after another with casual precision. The plasma gauntlet erupted again and again, sending gouts of blue fire into the ranks charging against him.*

*The air sang with the passage of high-velocity slivers; his armor reverberated agonizingly to their constant impact. The armor's bulk absorbed the impacts but transmitted the pain with seemingly perfect faithfulness: it felt as if he were walking barechested into a sandstorm.*

*He leaped and dodged forward, letting the armor pick its own targets and point his arm where it would, while he concentrated on evading the fire of the heavier weapons the Mishimans were bringing to bear. He ducked and* weaved between the seeking laser pulses, and if he could not evade them all, at least the gouges and scars they tore from the symbioplast armor were not fatal. And he loosed bursts of searing plasma from the gauntlet grown hot around his hand in endless series, seeking the men carrying the powerful man-portable missiles that could shatter armor and wearer alike.

He advanced through everything they threw at him, running, vaulting, firing, but for all his skill they hit him again and again. The power the armor diverted to healing its wounds was power denied to his weapons, and his telltales warned of less and less energy to call upon in either case, let alone both. Some of the plasma scars were too deeply etched to heal while he moved, breaking open again with each new exertion. And the building was still so far away....

The tank rose up out of the bunker, dwarfing him with its eighty-ton mass, the ground beneath torn and whirling at the interface point of its gravitic suspension field. He was too close to dodge and moving too quickly to stop—he struck the flank of the behemoth at full speed and bounced like a flung pebble. The tank seemed little inconvenienced.

He rolled aside as it turned ponderously, seeking to find him in its vision blocks. The laser in his hand fired steadily, forgotten in his stunned panic. It stitched half a dozen faint scars on the nuke-grade ablative cladding of hull and turrets. He flung a burst of plasma over his shoulder as he dodged, and it shredded and disappeared in the tank's magnetic shielding, full millimeters from the machine itself.

The tank was backing away now, its turrets traversing to sight on him. There was nothing he could do to prevent it, so his training turned him away, back toward the building. The range was extreme, perhaps even too great, but he had no more time. With a distant, drugged calmness he was aware of the turrets locking and the various weapons lowering to bear on him for a fatal volley.

He gave the command.

At once the legs of his suit locked rigidly in the preprogrammed stance. The torso of the armor bent him forward at the waist, to the angle calculated by the *ranging sensors built into his optics. The explosive bolts blew the bifurcated carapace away from his back.*

*And the missiles fired.*

*Immediately the two missiles cleared their racks, the armor completed its program, with a full-strength leap designed to throw him as far and fast as possible away from his frozen, vulnerable position. The tank's fire vaporized earth where he had posed the second before, and the building's defenses, directed skyward against the threats hurtling down from orbit, swiveled with cybernetic speed to meet this new danger.*

*Light.*

*Blinding burning glare beating through dark visor shadow.*

*Heat.*

*Mirrored protection evaporating from chest, arms, legs, helmet.*

*Wind.*

*The shock wave picked him up and tossed him like a chip adrift upon a torrent, hurling him back as though he weighed nothing, armor and all. He hit things: ground, wreckage, people, he never knew what; the nuclear gale plucked him free of each obstruction as casually as it had flung him against it. There was a sudden lapse of wind, as if he had fallen into the eye of a hurricane, and then the gale was back, rushing in the other direction to fill the space it had vacated. But Hallorhan had used the lull as best he could; he was flat against the ground, feet together, heels into the wind, armored fingers digging into the ruined ground like stakes. The backwave tore and plucked at him, and where he had hit things on the initial blast, now they hit him, as the loose detritus of the battlefield was drawn past him back toward the heart of the inferno.*

*The rush of displaced air passed, and Hallorhan cautiously raised his head. The field was still around him, swept clean of almost everything movable. The most prominent feature of the stripped landscape was the overturned, crippled tank.*

*There were two distinct craters at his ground zero; evidently the complex defenses had achieved that much success. But against even the low-yield tactical nukes, it hadn't made any difference. The building was gone, and without its warding sight the ships were descending now,* bright slivers flying unscathed through the desperate, undirected groundfire, to disgorge smaller ships that descended on the spaceport and deployed the marine infantry that would secure the city.

But none of that was Hallorhan's concern. He had achieved his objective, and in the achieving deprived himself of any set direction. The pills were beginning to wear off, the lead-limbed reaction setting in behind their chemical rush. The conditioning was still with him, full force, but without an objective it manifested itself only as an uneasy desire for movement, any movement.

The armor was stiff, awkward with all its scars and damage. The enerpacs were almost exhausted, he noticed for the first time; the armor must have drawn power like water through a hose to keep him alive through the detonation. Patiently, one foot after the other, he trudged away over the dead ground, in a direction he judged to be more or less upwind of the blast site.

The telltales read scarlet for every power system as he trudged up the gentle slope in the relatively unscarred greenbelt zone surrounding the city. Hallorhan didn't know where it was getting the energy to take each step as the armor bore him up the hill.

Finally he reached the shelter of the small clump of spruce that had been his goal, just below the crest of the hill. He put his back to a sapling, which bent alarmingly, and with infinite weariness slid heavily to the ground, looking back at the city he had helped level.

He had to laugh.

The thick mushroom pillar of his nukes rose from the pyre of the Mishiman command complex, dominating the scene like a spear haft plunged into a bed of coals. In the distance, in an expanding perimeter around the fallen spaceport, the Mishimans fought back with stubborn, foredoomed courage against the waves of marines debarking from each new squadron of landing cutters. But in between—

They radiated out like the fingers of a splayed hand, narrow ribbons of fire and destruction, each as wide as the zone of fire of a Special trooper, each completely independent of the other. Thin, pointless streamers of ruin *plunged into the meat of the city to no purpose and less effect.*

*The conditioning, Hallorhan realized, had worked perfectly. Attack, they had been told. Always advance, nothing can stop you. And nothing had. For long, straight, insanely perfect lines, the troopers of the Special company had charged ahead in a fury of superb skill and useless aggression, attacking with no thought for what they attacked until they were finally brought down or dropped in their tracks, power gone.*

*Now that he thought about it, he couldn't honestly remember whether he had followed the laid-out course to the objective himself, or if it had been blind fool's luck that let him accomplish his mission. The laughter was louder this time, as he decided he couldn't decide, a reaction to the waning powder-blue bouncers that finally broke over into hysterical tears. He laughed until he cried, laughed until his sides hurt, until he couldn't draw a breath and the armor's respiration monitors beeped warningly.*

*He reached up and activated his location beacon. He reached up and unlatched his visor, unsealed his breastplate to let the cool, fresh air reach his face and skin.*

*Then he sat back and waited for someone to come and tell him what to do.*

"Drop!" the senior drill shouted, and the ground came up to slap Hallorhan in the chest. The sound of the other trainees, the ones who were left, hitting the ground was lost in his own impact.

"Too slow! On your feet!" And Hallorhan was springing upward.

"Too slow! Drop!" The ground drove the wind from his lungs again. There was a way to catch yourself with your palms without being too obvious about it that took a lot of the impact off your chest, but the coordination to pull that off had gone about twenty drops ago.

"Too slow! On your feet!" Somewhere behind Hallorhan, a recruit moaned; elsewhere, another cursed. He could see the senior drill had heard them as well, and had to suppress a groan of his own. Complaining wasn't an option, and the drills would keep them dropping and

*recovering until either they learned to do it without com-
plaint or they were too winded to give voice.*

"Too slow! Drop!" *And Hallorhan hit the ground,
wordlessly.*

*The pain persisted now between the shocks.*

"You must understand us, Lieutenant," *the doctor-voice
came out of the air.* "We're not doing this simply to see you
suffer. But if you don't make any progress, we cannot in
good conscience turn you loose on an unsuspecting public.
They deserve better from us. You deserve better from us."

"So get them in here too," *Hallorhan muttered. He knew
from the pause that his comment had been noted, reported,
and probably recorded. But it wasn't acted upon, and he
was fast beginning to judge the validity of his actions by
how much current the taser balls arced through his body for
each mistake. He was still on his feet, so the hell with them.*

"Once more, please, Lieutenant."

*The street flashed into being around him again. Hallorhan
started the familiar walk. The hologram-pedestrian blundered
out of the doorway, the sandbag buffeted his shoulder. His
hands stayed at his side as he turned to face the door.
Another blow struck him high on the back from behind
and he drove an elbow straight back,* "through" *the face of
the drunk before the taser balls struck home and spasmed
him into the ground.*

"Guard that bag, trainee," *the senior drill said, dropping the small sandbag at Hallorhan's feet.* "I don't care
who tries to take it away from you, who orders you to give
it up, you keep that bag right there, you hear me?"

"Yes, Sergeant!"

"We'll see." *The senior drill moved to the recruits ringing in the pit. He pointed, and the first one jumped down
into the sawdust and started moving toward Hallorhan.*

*Five minutes later they had carried four trainees in
various states of disassembly out of the ring, and Hallorhan
had gone down under a solid wave of trainees and drills.
It took four men to get his fingers off the last trainee's
throat, and he was still trying to stuff the sandbag into his
mouth at the time.*

* * *

*He dropkicked the schoolboy with the errant football, and they shocked him flat.*

*They took them to the silhouette range and set them up on a course of fire, with five points for every silhouette hit and ten points lost for every round left in the magazine at the end of a series of targets. There were twelve targets, ten "hostiles" and two "noncombatants." There were eleven rounds in each magazine. A dead "noncombatant" meant five points off.*

*Hallorhan was the first recruit to figure out how to score a perfect 50.*

*The cat frisking around his legs got a broken spine. Hallorhan couldn't remember his name for five minutes when he came to.*

*They gave each of the recruits his or her own room in new barracks. Two of them together meant one or less alive after a night.*

*Hallorhan walked down the holographic street. "Citizens" jostled him, shouted at him, dropped things near him. Hallorhan's hands stayed at his side. But he killed each of them with his eyes, over and over. . . .*

*In the end, the drills and the doctors both got what they thought they wanted out of Deacon Hallorhan. They were both wrong.*

The wardroom chairs were beginning to feel more comfortable than his bunk, Hallorhan thought as he settled himself into his accustomed corner. At least he wasn't obliged to pay for the little rest he got there with memory.

The doctors had been thorough, in their limited way and to their limited ends. The only problem was, Deacon Hallorhan figured in those ways and ends only peripherally. In some ideal and impossible universe, a simple doctor had as his only goal the healing of his patients. But the only ideals in Fleet were the ideals Fleet issued you. Fleet doctors and therapists were military doctors and therapists . . . and a military doctor's first concern was not the cure of his patients, never had been.

A military doctor was there to keep personnel in usable condition for Fleet's use. Nothing else.

"*Have a seat, Lieutenant,*" the doctor said. He sounded like the voice that had goaded him again and again as he picked himself up off the "street," but that counted for nothing. They all sounded that way; they all adopted the same dry, casually tolerant bedside manner. They had picked it up in medical school, just as the recruits in training had come to ape the accents and mannerisms of the drills.

"Thank you, sir."

"*There's no need for such formality, Lieutenant. Under the circumstances I think we can safely dispense with it.*"

"Yes, s— all right," Hallorhan said. "Thanks."

Keep it informal, Lieutenant. *Let's pretend we're all equals here, Lieutenant . . . but on my terms,* Lieutenant. But Hallorhan knew better than to challenge the doctor at his little game. That was just the sort of thing they looked for, and Deacon Hallorhan was too quick a student to get caught that way ever again.

"*Sure.*" The doctor turned and keyed up Hallorhan's history on his desk 'bloc, as if it had only just occurred to him to study it. Hallorhan sat impassively as he read.

"*I'm glad we could have this little meeting, Lieutenant. For a while there, it looked like we wouldn't be able to.*"

"Yeah, well, I suppose I have been a little bit difficult to talk to lately."

The doctor chuckled paternally. "*Just a little. But you've come through that, Lieutenant, and we're all quite proud of the progress that's been made here—as you should be.*"

"If you say so."

The doctor switched off the 'bloc and swung back to face him. "*It hasn't been easy here, has it?*"

"I've been through worse."

"*Yes, I suppose you have. There've been a lot of changes because of the Specials, Lieutenant. You've blown up a lot of theories.*"

Actually, I blew up a lot of people, Hallorhan thought. You blew up the theories. All around.

"*They should have known better. You can't just pound*

*people into whatever shape and attitude you want from them, even if they agree to it. Between you and me, Lieutenant, there are times when I think the soldiers should stick to soldiering and stay the hell out of medicine."*

So should the doctors, Hallorhan thought, remembering the therapeutic bite of the taser balls. But he never said a word. Those long hours on the "street" had given him a control that could match any of the excesses the drills had unfolded in him, whenever he chose to use it.

"Anyway, I didn't call you in here just to browbeat you with my opinions of how the universe should be run," the doctor said. "I've got some more pertinent news. You're being processed for release, Lieutenant. You're good to go."

"I'm cured, sir?"

"Fully functional."

"I'm glad to hear that, sir, but—I still remember . . ."

"Of course you do, Lieutenant." The doctor's tone had sharpened somewhat. "We're not in the suppression business. Your mind is your own, Lieutenant; your memories are your own."

*You can have them!*

"Of course, sir."

"The important thing to remember is that we've given you the means to deal with those memories. You haven't had a lapse in the last dozen sessions. We think you can trust yourself in the outside world."

"Then I'm being sent back on duty?"

"No."

"Sir?"

"Lieutenant, you've given as much as the service can reasonably ask of you. You've earned your release."

"A medical?"

"Not at all. You've been authorized a fully honorable discharge, with an accompanying promotion to first lieutenant upon outprocessing. Congratulations. That should make a bit of a difference in your pension."

"Well, yes, sir, it should—but may I ask why I'm being favored this way? This doesn't seem to be the standard procedure for a psychological discharge."

"Why not? Don't you think you've earned it?" asked the

*doctor, who had never run through another man's charred guts.*

"*I wouldn't presume to say, sir.*"

"*Your case offers a number of exceptional considerations, Lieutenant. In retrospect, and in light of the unfortunate result, it has been determined that service in the Specials program very much constitutes service above and beyond the call, as it were. Compensation is called for. Unfortunately, the circumstances of the service bar any more official notice. So we're doing the best we can by you through administrative procedures.*"

In other words, they were trying to ease him out as quietly as possible, and all their little rewards were a candy-coating to keep him quiet about it. Well, he'd oblige them. He was too aware that they could just as easily bottle him up somewhere for the rest of his life. Maybe they actually *did* feel *some* guilt, some obligation to set things right by him. He certainly wouldn't turn them down.

"*I appreciate that, sir.*"

"*I'm glad to hear that. The important thing to remember, Lieutenant, is that we've done everything we can for you, Lieutenant, and that's quite a lot. The rest is up to you now. We're sure you won't disappoint us.*"

"*I don't intend to, sir.*"

"*Good.*" Hallorhan found himself automatically accepting the hand the doctor proffered. "*I won't keep you any longer, Lieutenant. If you'll go along to personnel, they'll get your release under way.*"

"*Thank you, sir.*" Hallorhan rose and left the office.

They ran him through the administrative maze with admirable speed and an impersonality that he found refreshing after the doctor's clinical bonhomie. It took them less than two hours to terminate an enlistment of six years, and he found himself out on the street, literally and figuratively, with a pension and a pocketful of standards and the memory of a burning city. . . .

The only thing they had given him that he valued was his control, and he knew that they had done that entirely for their own convenience. But he could use it, and he would, for as long as it mattered.

* * *

"I didn't mean to wake you," Mitsuko said.

"I wasn't asleep," Hallorhan said, opening his eyes. "What are you doing here?"

"I wasn't asleep either," Mitsuko said. "I thought I might as well not be asleep here. It's quieter."

"If you say so."

He plainly didn't mean to say anything further. Mitsuko sat there with him, surrounding herself with his silence. But something was happening, something new to her. Hallorhan's telepathic silence was a balm to her, without question—but as she grew familiar with it, she began to sense a lack, an emptiness to it that she couldn't define. It didn't *bother* her, nothing like that. Yet she felt as if there were something she should have been getting from it that just wasn't there. Had she been able to admit it to herself, she might have realized that she had lived too long with the minds of everyone around her for their absence to be an easy state, however necessary to her.

"Why are you always in here?" she asked.

"Where should I be?"

"Don't you ever sleep?"

He shook his head. "Not if I can avoid it. It's too crowded in there."

"You mean what Moses calls your old war stories?"

"He told you about that?"

"I know what goes on aboard my ship," Mitsuko said. "I know Moses thinks I don't do anything but hide under a rock down in engineering, but I keep in touch."

"Good for you," Hallorhan said.

"I mean, I have to, don't I?" She scowled, seeming to forget him for a moment. "There seem to be a great many things one *has* to do. Everyone has their little demands, don't they?"

"So I've noticed," Hallorhan said. "It gets to the point where I wonder sometimes if it's worth the effort of humoring them."

Mitsuko laughed humorlessly. "It may as well be. They always have a great big stick to back up their little demands, and just a tiny bit of carrot that's meant to take the sting out of being driven." She looked at him. "Except you."

"Except me what?"

"You don't make any demands, Deacon."

"Should I?"

"I'd rather you didn't. It makes a change."

"Whatever you want."

"It's been a while since I heard that. Thank you."

"Glad to oblige." They sat in silence for a moment, as he grew increasingly aware of her continued scrutiny. "May I impose to the extent of asking a question?"

"All right," Mitsuko said warily.

"Why are *you* always in here? Don't *you* ever sleep?"

"That's two questions."

"You're absolutely right. Fair's fair, answer whichever one you like."

"You're a man of your word, sir."

"It goes with being an ex-officer and former gentleman."

"First time I'd ever noticed it. Anyway, to answer your question . . . well, as you said, it's too crowded in there."

"There seems to be a lot of that going around."

"Doesn't there, though. It's practically an epidemic."

"Practically. The only thing worse than the disease might be the cure."

"What's that?"

"Not being useful. Not being necessary. If you haven't got anything they want, they won't demand it of you."

"That might do it, but you'd have to put a hell of a lot of work into not being worth anything to anybody. I mean, you'd never know what they might want from you."

"I never said it would be easy," Hallorhan said. "Being worthless is a full-time job."

"And like you said, it gets to the point where you wonder if it's worth it."

"Sometimes."

"More and more and more," Mitsuko said.

"There's just one thing you want to remember, though," Hallorhan said.

"What's that?"

"The only way to beat their demands is to make demands of your own. And then that's on *your* head. That's the scary part. If you have a desire, you're responsible for its result."

"I think I'd chance it."

"Do you think I would?"

"I don't know what you think, Deacon."

"Well, that makes two of us."


At first she thought the flight deck was empty when she entered. There was no sign of Moses' familiar bulk rising up from the captain's station, no one greeted her as she came in.

Then she saw him.

For a moment she thought she was looking at a different person. Moses was unchanged physically, although the way he slouched in his seat was drastically atypical of him. He was bent almost double, resting his head on one arm atop the covered keyboard. But the fear he radiated was like nothing she had ever felt from him before, a shrill overtone that made of his thoughts a twisted muddle, difficult to read—and probably just as bad to live inside.

"Moses? Captain, are you all right?"

He jerked his head up from his arm at her voice. He looked around at her, and for a moment she felt something redder, anger or resentment, pierce through the discoloring fear.

"Spooky."

"Are you all right?"

"What the hell are you doing here? It isn't your watch."

"I know." How to explain that she had followed an unfamiliar effluvium of terror to its source, without explaining either how she had recognized it and whom she had recognized it in? "I just thought I'd come up."

"You never just come up."

"Well, I did this time, dammit."

"Good for you."

"What's wrong, Moses?"

"Nothing's wrong—hell, *everything's* wrong. I don't know what happened. I was standing my watch. I was looking out the port, and all of a sudden, I was scared of the stars. Do you believe that? When was I ever scared to look out a damned porthole?"

"You never were, Moses." She knew his star-gazing for one of his few pleasures. "I thought you liked it."

"Yes, well, not this time. I was looking out there, and I just suddenly thought, 'How empty is it; how easy it would be to just let it swallow me up.'" The anger thickened. It could not diminish the fear, but it shunted it aside. "Dammit, Spooky, nothing's going to swallow me up! What could I have been thinking of?"

"You've got a lot to worry about, Moses. The killing, the trigger—"

"The hell with that! I've had worries before, Spooky, and I never let them get to me like that!"

"Then I wouldn't worry about it," Mitsuko said. "It's probably just something that snuck up on you . . ."

"Nothing sneaks up on me. Not twice, anyway."

"Then it's probably finished. Give me the board, go pour yourself a stiff drink and go to bed."

"Now there's a prescription I can live with." Moses paused. "Is Hallorhan still in there?"

"He was when I left."

"Good. The stars may be too big for me to face up to anymore, but his ass I can chew." And he left, the memory of his fear already fading in the face of more pragmatic irritations.

But Mitsuko's fear was strong in her again, because she had looked into that fear while it dominated him, and the spider at the center of that web of alarm wore James Emerson White's face.

# CHAPTER 9

"Let me face him," Mitsuko demanded.

"This is quite a reversal," Eisberg answered her. "Weren't you the person who was so stubborn about taking my instruction?"

"That was different. That was just you and me. I didn't want to do your dirty work for you. But now he's hurting people who can't fight back."

"He's been doing that all his life, to a great many more people than your tatty little space-captain."

"I didn't know them."

"And that makes it all right, does it? What a callous, self-serving attitude—"

"Are you going to sit there joking or are you going to show me how to fight this bastard?"

"I've had nothing else in mind since your lessons started," the nodality responded. "Indeed, you might say I live for nothing else." He looked around, wistfully. "If one can call this living. But as for fighting James Emerson White—no. Not now."

"*Now* is when I have to!"

"*Now* is when you're not ready. If you were to fight him, at your present level of skill—forgive my perversion of the term—you would lose. You could not help your friends now, and ultimately you could not protect them at all. That is what we're discussing here, isn't it?"

"That's what I'm talking about. I haven't got the slightest idea what your priorities are—except that they have to stink."

"Whatever my priorities, our ends are the same. Accept

that for now and you might actually learn enough to survive. Now then—"

The darkness was back—but this time there was a difference. Mitsuko could feel herself moving already, not of her own volition but trapped in some great and swirling current that bore her away at an impossible speed and in so many different directions that she swiftly lost all track of her progress, save for the baseless certainty that she was being drawn downward, pulled ever deeper into the black limbo that engulfed her.

Then the current was gone, as swiftly as it had appeared, and Mitsuko Tamura was left alone again in the unseen, unfelt, unheard emptiness she had come to hate as deeply as she hated the mocking Eisberg. At once she drew on the rage that sustained and began to move back the way she had come. Faster and faster she sped, moving with such intended, if unseen, velocity that it seemed impossible for the murk to sustain her. For all Eisberg's cool contempt for her, Mitsuko was a quick study: introduced to the possibility of movement through the void, she had grasped the practice of it at once. And as she flew, forward and upward with all the speed she could muster, she expanded her awareness of herself outward as she had been taught, wider and wider, seeking to drive back the darkness and reveal her hidden baiter once again.

There was nothing there. Nothing. No one.

She lost track of the time as she flew onward. It could have been minutes, seconds, hours, an eternity trapped within the confines of her skull. Her anger, which she had thought a limitless quality with which she could fill the whole of the night around her, began to pale, insufficient to conquer the blackness. And as the anger waned the fear began to replace it, the helpless, draining awareness of her manipulability by forces that she did not understand, that she feared.

She slowed in her mad flight, seeking to conserve the energy of her anger, but the fear that suggested such husbanding drained away more strength than was saved. Her awareness, driven outward like an enormous crystal sphere that encompassed only emptiness, began to contract almost of its own accord, drawn in by its own trepidation.

Finally, she simply hung there, a single mote of self in a continuum that had no place for it. She imagined she felt a growing cold, and chided herself for the thought; she was possessed of no form, not even in analogue, vulnerable to such a sensation. But the feeling persisted, as did the impression that the darkness around her was still slowly compressing the small node of awareness she had withdrawn into, by its sheer obsidian presence.

Then, somehow, she became aware of a direction—no, barely a hint of a path—that beckoned her to follow. For a moment she hesitated, for the mass of the darkness around her oppressed her spirit entirely. But reason still existed, and she could see no point in remaining where she was, in whatever sense that concept had value. With a single, convulsive effort she uncoiled in the direction of the sensation—

—and fell heavily to the acrebeast carpet, as if at the end of a desperate leap.

Eisberg seemed singularly unmoved by her exertions.

"And you were ready to fight for your life?" he asked, and for all that he never raised his voice, he made it sound like the most ludicrous notion he had ever encountered and only she could have been foolish enough to have given voice to it. "You have too much yet to learn even to question the course of your education, and I frankly begin to doubt that you are capable of mastering it in time."

"Then quit, why don't you?" Mitsuko challenged him. The warmth of the study around her and the acrebeast carpet against her legs were a blessing untainted even by Eisberg's presence.

"I'm afraid I cannot entertain the notion, much as it might please me. That is not my purpose here."

"To hell with your purpose—" but she was talking to the darkness, which swept her up and carried her away again.

She felt a blinding mixture of panic and rage. Eisberg had never subjected her to two sessions one immediately after the other; hadn't he seen the trouble she had had with the last one? The prospect of rushing futilely through the darkness with the waiting cold hovering behind her again was a specter that haunted her too closely to be borne.

She wanted *out*. Away from the darkness, away from

Eisberg, *away*. She retreated from the darkness, remembering the worn, warm familiarity of the *Wild Goose*, the familiar texture of the tech-pit seat beneath her, the flickerings and chimings of her undemanding boards—

—and they were in front of her, solid and substantial, the cushions real beneath her and the keyboard tangible under her hands. Although it had felt like forever, the chronometer before her showed that her passage through limbo and Eisberg's hands had lasted less than ten minutes.

She suddenly realized she was not alone on the flight deck. Eisberg was there, glaring at her from the captain's station. She knew it was significant, somehow, that he had not drawn her back to his study again—but the anger on his face meant even more.

"And just what the hell did you think you were doing?"

"I left. I'd had enough of your teaching for one day."

"You left. . . . You don't understand, do you? You don't realize what a risk you took."

"What risk did I take? By not trotting meekly back to you in your little nook before you graciously consented to send me back out here where I belonged? What sort of risk was I taking?"

"You don't understand the dangers of the dark. It's so terribly easy to get lost down there, lost forever—"

"I knew where I wanted to go." Understanding struck her. "That's what you don't want me to realize, isn't it? That I didn't *have* to come back to you to find my way out. I've learned something you didn't want me to know, haven't I? Why not, Eisberg? Why shouldn't I know that I can find my own way out of the dark?"

"It's not as easy as you think."

"I'll just bet it isn't. It isn't just finding my own way, is it? You don't want me learning *anything* you didn't show me. Why not? Why do you have to be involved in everything I know? Why does everything have to be routed through you?"

"Because you don't know what to look for, what the limits of the talent are."

"I don't know what *your* limits are."

"They're well beyond any capability you've displayed so far."

"Yes, O, Great and Powerful Oz. Whatever you say."

"Don't be flip. You need me."

"Wrong. I need what you know, to get out of this mess you've got me in. And as far as that goes, you need me, to solve your problem. So let's dispense with this master-and-novice garbage and try a little honesty for a change. I know it's out of character, but give it a whirl. You never know, you might like it."

Eisberg grimaced ill-humoredly. "All right. What do you think you should know?"

"Just for starters, how this convenient situation came about. How did White know where to find the trigger?"

"White *doesn't* know. It was discovered by his nodality, being carried by Captain Orange. White won't even know about his new toy until you arrive off Avalon."

"That doesn't wash. How did the *nodality* know where to find the trigger?"

"White sends his doppelgangers out routinely, looking for situations of profit and advantage. He's quite active in that area. That's how we discovered him."

"Uh-huh. So the White nodality just happened to be on Hybreasil when Jakubowski obtained the trigger, and just couldn't resist the chance to pick it up for his toy chest?"

"Essentially. That is, after all, the purpose of White's nodalities."

"It's also too damned pat an answer. Especially when the Institute is involved. Do you expect me to believe you people didn't sort of accidentally deliberately let him learn about the trigger, to draw him out and mix me up with him?"

"It's not an unreasonable speculation on your part, based on your opinion of us, I suppose."

"You suppose. Fine. Now here comes the interesting question: how long have you been leaning on Moses Callahan, to get him to come back to where you could get at me?"

"That was purely good fortune—"

"'We've kept track of you since Proxima Wentworth,' remember? You've got to learn to keep your lies in order. Independents hardly ever come back in toward Confederate center, and you know it. You wouldn't have left it to chance that I'd show up when you needed a warm body on hand, would you? No answer? This has been quite a little project for you people, hasn't it? White *and* me, all in one tidy lump. And to do it you got Axyll Jakubowski killed and you've been playing games inside my captain's head, for how long?"

"I've been dedicated to this project for two years. I don't know what else has been involved." He attempted a smile. "I'm hardly in a position to find out myself."

"Two years. At least. No wonder Moses is a nervous wreck. You've been twisting his life all out of shape for two damned years, just to get at me. I underestimate you people sometimes, I really do."

"Those decisions are not my province."

"You only exist because of those decisions. You don't get off that easily." With an effort, Mitsuko restrained her temper. "Shit. All right, a more immediately practical question: why is White leaving me alone?"

"He presumes he got the measure of you that day when he came aboard."

"He must not think much of you as a teacher."

"He isn't aware of me. There is no way he could be. In terms of nodal sentience, I am a much more limited construct than he is. His nodality has to be allowed considerable leeway of action to function as he wishes it to. Also, he is not that skilled at nodal mechanics. I am simply an instructional matrix. I have no existence outside the awareness of my carrier. When I am not active, he cannot detect me, for there is nothing to set me apart from the run of your memories."

"And when you are active? What happens if he catches me when I'm blundering around down in the dark next time?"

"He will not. I have been careful to offer you instruction only when Captain Orange is asleep. He cannot perceive anything without an aware carrier."

"So why don't I just smother him with a pillow while he's asleep?"

"Why don't you?"

"I've been around you too long. I almost had to stop and think of an answer for that. Aside from the practical considerations that he's going to have people waiting for him when he gets to Avalon, I'm not a murderer. Yet."

"A pity. A certain callousness would be a useful attribute just now."

"No, it wouldn't. If I had it, you'd be dead by now, or dissolved, or whatever it is nodalities do."

"If you could manage it."

"Try me."

"Don't get overconfident. You've put me at a disadvantage, true, but you've hardly reversed our roles yet. There's still a great deal to learn, and you still need me to teach you." Eisberg grinned. "Oh, you *are* learning, after all. Not one recrimination about how you wouldn't need to learn it if it weren't for us, this time. Very good. And so, onward."

"One last question."

"What?"

"Deacon Hallorhan."

"The pilot."

"The pilot. Why can't I hear him?"

"Can't you?" Eisberg looked off to one side for a moment. "Why no, you can't, can you? That's very interesting. I've never encountered anything like that, myself."

"How about that? Something you don't know."

"I never said that. I said I'd never *encountered* it. Please remember my personal limitations. As it happens, I'm not unfamiliar with the phenomenon. There are generally two causes of this silence in the ungifted: direct tissue damage to elements of the right side of the brain that have been determined to participate in the propagation of telepathic sendings, or a rigorous history of behavioristic psychological conditioning. Since your pilot appears to have most of his head intact, I have to assume that in this case it is the latter."

"That fits. Not that I want to, by any means, but is there any way to break that conditioning?"

"I rather hope not. The nature of the therapy required to produce the effect is particularly severe. Whatever it was that was deemed necessary to be locked up in that fashion is probably not something I would want to see running around loose."

*He's stronger than I thought he would be.*

"Why are you surprised?" Luther Orange asked tiredly. "He's a captain. That calls for a certain degree of character."

*I am conversant with the merits of captains, "Captain."*

"No, you're not," Luther Orange said. "You're familiar with me. I'm an ex-captain. A bankrupt captain. Moses Callahan is a captain who has kept his ship. There's a difference. A big difference."

*Not much of a one. He frightens easily.*

"Of course he does. He's going his own way. Anyone like that scares easily. But he doesn't quit so readily, does he?"

*He will. And you will help him do so. After all, this will be your ship when he gives it up.*

"Damn you, I do my job for you already—"

*Your job is what I decide it is, "Captain."*

"I could like this man."

*I cannot use him. Think about it.*

"What more can I do? I've talked to him already. He's heard everything I can say."

*You can show me what a captain fears.*

*The landscape was dead all around him.*

*The prairie stretched out in all directions, flat and featureless, sere brown grass rustling in the faint wind. Overhead the sky was an inverted bowl of limitless depth, of a blue that deepened almost to indigo the more nearly vertical one looked.*

*Moses hated it. The grass shifted beneath his feet like a poorly woven straw mat, cutting him off from the soil underneath. The sun was an actinic coin, high in the impossibly blue sky, that scored the back of his neck like a brand. The unending, dun boredom of the scene before him seemed a weight on his eyes, bending his head until the scope of his vision encompassed the brittle grass before him, no different from the grass a foot away or a hundred feet away or a hundred miles away. The heat and the dryness and the bright daylight were entirely different, but there was something about the scene that reminded him of home, of nighean aig Donnegal back on Og Eirrin.*

*The emptiness. That was it. The constant, unchanging, everlasting emptiness of the landscape matched anything his natal world could offer him.*

*On an impulse he turned and started walking. Soon he found himself ascending a shallow slope the uniform color and verdure of the terrain had masked. He ascended it*

higher than he would have thought possible for such a
hidden hill, and then he was at the crest and looking
down.

The ship rested in the shallow valley, a blunt gunmetal
wedge squatting on its landing gear. The Wild Goose
seemed impatient, as if it longed to be free of this confin-
ing, dull world as badly as he did but lacked the spark of
will that would bid it depart.

Moses started down the slope toward the ship, slowly at
first, picking his footing carefully in the matted grass, but
gradually yielding to the pull of gravity, running clumsily
down the hill with all the speed the slope and his legs
could give him. The thick grass snagged and pulled at his
feet, so that more than once he stumbled and almost fell,
but it could not hold him back. The hatch to the Wild
Goose stood open and beckoning, and Moses answered the
call.

The hatch boomed shut behind him in a way he had
never known it to do before, and he was back within the
comforting, limiting walls of steel that he sought so strongly.

He made his way to the flight deck, and the instruments
flickered and beeped at him with a vividness he would not
have thought them capable of at their advanced age. He
turned and looked down into the tech pit, where Spooky
looked back up at him with eyes that shone like a lemur's,
wide and vulnerable and trusting. The pilot's station was
empty, as it had been in the good times, and Moses swung
himself into the seat with a youthful ease of distant
memory.

The ship trembled around him as he brought the fans up
to speed. He fed in more power and let up on the brakes,
and the Wild Goose clawed its way into the sky like a
pursuit ship. Like an arrow the old tramp climbed out,
seeking the indigo sky overhead and cleaving it in search
of stars.

The dry, barren, deadening world that was all the
worlds Moses Callahan had ever left behind fell away
beneath the ship as he cut in the light drive and the Wild
Goose aimed its mad rush at the stars.

Moses moved to the captain's station, unlocking the
vector-shift board. With practiced, assured ease, he dialed
up the coordinates of a target system and keyed in the

shift. Around the ship the stars snapshifted, like a jump cut in a popcart scene, and the small globe of a world appeared ahead of them. With a speed like none he had ever experienced before, Moses brought the Goose flaming down into the atmosphere—

—and found himself cruising over a sea of sere brown grass.

He stared at it, puzzled, as the ship flew on over hundreds of kilometers of unchanging grasslands. Finally, baffled, he pulled back on the stick and the ship climbed smoothly out again, into the welcoming blackness of space. Again he moved to the vector-shift board and summoned up a world—

—and again he found himself flying over a sea of grass. Sterile, useless, profitless grass.

He felt a new presence at his shoulder and looked up. It was Hallorhan, and something deep in those hooded, noncommittal eyes drained youth and vigor from Moses in one long pull. As though someone else were working his limbs, he stood up from the pilot's station, edging aside as the younger man slid in behind the controls. Moses turned for the captain's station, and as he did he met Mitsuko's stare, wounded and unhappy, as though he'd betrayed her.

He reached for the board and froze, hands suspended over the keys as Hallorhan pulled the ship up easily from the brown world and back into space. The stars seemed to gleam now with a cold, indifferent hostility.

He looked down at the shift board again, at the planet codes scrolling up over his screen there. He was filled with a sudden, unnameable fear, a certainty that much would rest on his next choice that he would rather not risk. But the choice was not his. Almost at random, he selected a world and keyed it in. He initiated the shift—

—and they were flying over grass once again.

Without a word, Hallorhan was rising up out of the pilot's station and reaching for him. Seized with a terror beyond expression, Moses struck at the pilot with a fist that he pulled back wrinkled and lined with sudden age. He lurched away from Hallorhan and recoiled, to feel Mitsuko's hands upon his shoulders like claws of ice-clad steel. He turned and scrambled for the hatch, looking back at them in the unending second it took to cycle open.

Mitsuko looked back at him with enormous eyes, as black as the space they traveled, that shone at him like the bright, cold stars. Then he was through the hatch and running, running.

The master's cabin flooded the corridor with dust as he opened the door. Through the swirling gray clouds Moses saw a big, sandy-haired young man in the uniform of a corporate-line junior officer straighten up over the dusty, emaciated corpse with the four gold braids on his sleeve. The young man looked at him with the eyes Moses Callahan had looked out of thirty years before and began to approach him. Moses retreated into the hallway, and with Hallorhan's hand upon his shoulder feeling like an iron spike driven through his heart, Moses half-fought, half-fell free and ran again.

The smell from the holds drove him back, an impenetrable foulness, the pallets heaped high with rancid dross and offal. It was a smell of cesspools, of charnel houses, of years of profitless dealing. There was no place left to run.

They caught him up and pulled him away from the holds. He struggled and twisted but Mitsuko and Hallorhan gripped him firmly, and the strength he had known all his life deserted him in an instant. He felt light, insubstantial, helpless. But in his struggles he managed to turn for a final glimpse of the holds as his younger self cycled the hatch back shut, and gold gleamed at him through the forever-barred doorway as the hatch rammed home.

Then they were bearing him toward the passenger access hatch, and somehow he was naked between them. His wrinkled old man's body humiliated him, but it was only a minor indignity beside his mounting horror.

The hatch opened onto a vista of brown grass (when had they landed?). Moses made a final, despairing struggle, keening like a frightened child, but they paid him no attention. They bundled him out the door, and the grass rasped and cut him as he landed. There was a great wind upon his back as he rose to his knees and stood, and by the time he had turned the Wild Goose was a dwindling speck in the perfect sky. He ran after it, screaming, cursing, pleading, but the widening vapor trail of the freighter never wavered, never bent as it indicated its irrevocable

*departure, leaving the sick old man alone upon the prairie
beneath it....*

"Shit."

Hallorhan looked up curiously as Moses came onto the
flight deck. Moses squinted against the glare of the dialed-
up illumination and turned to see Mitsuko looking up, face
drawn and tense, over the edge of the tech pit.

"Goddammit," Moses said. "Isn't there any place a man
can go to *not* sleep in privacy anymore?"

# CHAPTER 10

It was such a small thing to have caused so much trouble, really.

Moses looked down at the crated trigger, sitting on its lashed-down pallet apart from the rest of the cargo in the shadowed hold, and there was nothing he wanted more than simply to jettison it, throw it overboard to drift forever harmless in the outer tracks of the Hybreasil system.

But no sooner had the thought shaped itself than the sensation with which he had become only too familiar returned. Whatever he wanted made no difference. He was too old, too weak, too frightened to take any action in the matter. He had been forced into taking the cargo because he was over the hill as a trader, couldn't pay his way without it, and to have refused might have cost him his ship. He would deliver his cargo, because not to do so would expose him to the rage and retaliation of Fleet for leaving such a danger floating around loose, or the League, outraged at the might he had cost them, or Luther Orange's unseen employers. And for some reason he could not explain, this last prospect frightened him most of all.

The access hatch to the holds opened, transfixing him with a plane of light. Luther Orange's shadow was a black finger that reached down and touched him between the shoulder blades.

"I thought I denied you permission to come in here," Moses said. Luther Orange continued to walk down the narrow track of light as assuredly as if he owned the place.

"No, you didn't," he answered. "What you said was, you

didn't think access to the holds would be possible. But here I am, so I guess it was."

"Get out," Moses Callahan said plainly. But he wasn't surprised when Luther Orange ignored him, to look down on the trigger himself.

"It's amazing the lengths people will go to in order to obtain such power," he said. "I'd hate to run the risk of bringing that sort of ambition down on my head."

"I never wanted to be obliged to."

"Then don't be, man. Come in with us. We can use you."

"That's just what I'm afraid of. I don't want to be usable, not to anyone who could want something like this."

"Everyone is usable, Captain. To someone or the other. But if we're lucky, some of us can pick by whom and on what terms we're used."

"Can we, now? And did you get the terms you wanted?"

"I'm happy with my situation."

"Meaning you didn't. And you can't hope for better, in spite of your accommodation."

"That's not entirely true, Captain. I have every hope of a change in my fortunes shortly."

"Lucky fellow. How?"

"A ship." He met Moses' stricken look. "The *Goose*."

"Do they really think I'll give her up?"

"Do you really think you can keep them from taking her?"

"Damned straight," he said, but the words sounded hollow even to him, with the crated evidence of Orange's unseen masters' skill at acquisition hard by his side.

"You're probably right—if you use some sense," Luther Orange said.

"What do you mean?"

"They need a ship. They'll give it to me because I'm a certified captain. But if you volunteered to provide them with a ship, *you* could make a case for remaining as master aboard. What it reduces to is, if they have to *take* the *Goose* from you, they'll give her to me, but if you *offer* them the ship, they might let you keep her."

"And if you thought there was the least damned chance of that, you'd never have made the suggestion, now, would you?"

Luther Orange shrugged. "It isn't as if you have a great many options left, Captain. I merely suggested the best outcome you could hope for, as a professional courtesy. I've been where you're headed, and I wouldn't much like to see you go through what I went through."

"Get the hell away from me," Moses said, stepping toward the other man. But even as he felt the anger rise within him, a new wave of the fear and weakness washed over him, drowning it in cold apprehension. And most humiliating of all, from the look on Luther Orange's face, he knew that it was there as well.

*Weak old man...*

"I've done you as much of a favor as I can, Captain," Luther said. "You're right; I want a ship, and if I can get this ship, I'll take her. But I had to give you the chance to make the offer."

"Make it to whom?" *Tired old man...*

"You'll find that out when we reach Avalon."

*Useless old man...*

"I'm not hypocritical enough to wish you luck, Captain, so good day." He turned and walked back up the light, which vanished as the hatch shut behind him, leaving Moses in the shadows, staring helplessly down at his free-on-board bane.

"Do you think he'll come around?" Nullman asked eagerly.

"Yes," Luther Orange said. "Yes, I think he will." The thought gave him no satisfaction, for all that he desired just that result most dearly.

*Your guilt does you credit, "Captain." You are a good man, aren't you?*

"Our own ship," Nullman said. "What we couldn't do then."

*Yes, it does open up one's prospects, doesn't it—within certain limits, of course.*

"What about crew, though? We'd need crew. Do you think the ones aboard now would stay on?"

*Now that will be a problem, "Captain." We cannot use these people, in spite of your kind suggestion to Captain Callahan. The woman has a talent I mistrust, however easily I can overmaster it. And the pilot—the pilot is a puzzle to me, and I do not care for puzzles.*

*I shall have to make arrangements.*

"They probably won't want to," Luther Orange said.

"Well, that's no good, is it?" Nullman said. "I mean, they know about us, don't they? We can't leave them running around loose. We'll have to take care of them."

Two lousy backshootings, Luther Orange thought, and he's coming on like a popcart beamslinger.

"I wish I still had my laser. We'll need it, won't we? I wonder if we can get it back?"

"I imagine if we need it, I can get hold of it," Luther Orange said.

*Then we had best get hold of it, "Captain."*

"There'll be time enough after we've shifted," Luther Orange assured them both. "We may as well let them take care of the delicate work first."

Moses hesitated over the board, chilled by a sudden memory of waving grass. The image came through to Mitsuko as clearly as a painting, framed in Moses' surging fear.

"Everything's set here, Moses," she prodded him, and felt the fear's hold jarred by the intrusion and the reminder of his responsibilities. The picture of the brown plain vanished from his mind and her sight.

"Good," he said. "Get ready to load destination."

"Open and waiting."

Moses called up the chart indexes and ran down the lists to the series code for Avalon. "Input up."

"Loading. Accessed."

"Load departure point."

"Confirmed and loaded. Accessed."

"Load plotted course from departure point."

"Confirmed and loaded. Accessed."

"Load observed course from departure point."

"Confirmed and loaded. Accessed and correlated."

"Vector-shift assembly status."

"Status optimal, green board. I knew those cabin-head gasket seals would come in good for something."

"Ha bloody ha. Stick to the drill please; I don't feel like discovering a new vector by accident just today."

"Status optimal, green board, Captain."

"Thank you." He reached forward and unlocked the transparent cover to the vector-shift trigger. "Shifting now."

He thumbed down the flashing scarlet button and the *Wild Goose* fell out of space, tumbling off the familiar curve generated by the mass of the universe onto a shorter path between two points that might never otherwise have met. Outside, the stars flickered and snapped into new constellations. There were too many of the distant, fiery suns by far to follow the exact pattern of the shift: there was instead simply an abrupt and disturbing awareness of difference that was perhaps more alarming than any perceived movement might have been.

"Shift confirmed," Moses stated. "Going for position—got it. A three-beacon fix. At least we're on the right side of the sun."

"What's our ETA, Captain?" Mitsuko asked.

"Board shows seven days."

"Damn."

"The hell with that. Set up for a corrective shift."

"Input up."

"Load point location determined by beacon fix."

"Confirmed and loaded. Accessed."

"Plotted course, same. Observed course, same."

"Confirmed. Accessed and correlated."

"Generating new destination by extrapolated beacon fix. Load."

"Confirmed and loaded. Accessed."

"Shifting now." Again the stars spasmed, jewels shaken upon an ebony rug. "Shift confirmed. Revised ETA, three shipboard days."

Moses lowered the shift trigger cover and locked it back in place. "Board locked and cleared. Pilot, the ship is yours. Or whoever the hell thinks they want it."

"I have the ship, Captain."

"Avalon Highside should be answering our ID broadcast in an hour or so."

"Aye aye, sir. Do you wish to be notified?"

"No, I don't see the point. Just log whatever braking and approach orders they give you and execute them."

"Yes, sir. When should we yell for Fleet?"

"The sooner we get rid of that damned thing the better—" *No*, the thought struck him with the weight of a blow, and the fear was strong behind it. "—but we can't risk a broadcast. There's no telling who might hear it, and it's a long way to Avalon yet. I'd feel better waiting until we're grounded and set in the middle of the port." The truth of the matter was that Moses doubted he would ever feel better again, but as he spoke he felt the weight of the fear lessening, to be replaced by a scarcely felt emotion that might almost have been satisfaction. But hardly his.

He was suddenly aware of his crew watching him, with eyes out of a nightmare. "Dammit, we're not going to advertise our troubles to everyone and his nephew until we're in a position to do something about them."

Hallorhan shrugged and acquiesced. "Aye, aye, sir."

Mitsuko stared at him a moment longer, then started to climb out of the tech pit. "I'm going to lock the shift assembly on standby."

"You can do that from here."

"I can do that aft, too, Captain." And she was gone.

"It's all yours, Mr. Hallorhan."

"Yes, sir."

Luther Orange found him in the master's cabin. "I came by to pick up our secured effects, Captain."

"What secured effects?" Moses asked. He had been studying the hand holding the glass before him, unexpectedly fascinated by how seamed and weathered, how *worn*, it had become without his noticing. When had that had time to happen?

"You have some of Mr. Nullman's property."

The laser. "I won't have passengers aboard my ship wandering around with weapons.

"Be reasonable, Captain. You're insystem and broadcasting your identification and registry already. We're not about to start shooting people. We'd have a hell of a time explaining it to the port, wouldn't we?"

"Then what do you want it for?" The lassitude was settling over him again in a crippling fog, but the laser was too obvious a danger for him to dismiss, even with White's unknown encouragement.

"Because it's our property. And because it's an option we have, whether we want to exercise it or not."

"Options are nice things."

"So would you please open the safe and let me have it?"

Moses wouldn't have thought the helplessness could get any worse. He was wrong. The urge was overwhelming to acquiesce, to avoid the difficulty of resisting. But the danger was simply too overt.

"Be damned to you. Get it yourself if you want it."

And he wasn't surprised when Luther Orange went to the safe, which he shouldn't have been able to find, and opened it just like that, with the combination he shouldn't have known. He lifted out the laser and the magazine Moses had drawn from its butt, with its double column of disposable enerpacs and fluoride cartridges. He slipped the magazine back into the well and pocketed the weapon, while Moses just sat there, the enormity of his impotence weighing him down like chains.

"We haven't the time I thought we'd have," Eisberg told her pettishly.

"After all your planning, too," she consoled him mockingly.

"You're in no position to joke," he said crossly. "There are things you *have* to know, and you will have to assume the burden of learning them much more rapidly than I would have been comfortable with."

"Of course I will. You people don't work any other way. All right. Give it your best shot."

She wasn't down in the dark three seconds before she restored herself to her cabin. "I've seen that already," she said, when Eisberg manifested himself.

"We won't get anywhere if you insist on disrupting the instruction."

"Then show me something new—" She was back in the darkness, and this time the currents were a raging flood that threatened to sweep her away into infinite night. But their violence was a difference only of degree, not kind, and she swiftly righted herself and surged back toward her cabin and the real world—

—only to find herself suddenly on the flight deck.

Astonished, she looked down at the board before her— and at the two square, seamed, masculine hands that rested there. Even as that shock registered she felt the second awareness, Moses' awareness, cohabiting her mind in numb amazement— no, she was invading *his*, she realized. She tried to pull back, to withdraw, but Eisberg held her there, or tried to: she felt her mind stretching like taffy. Then she could perceive her cabin around her again—while the flight deck was still clear before her, and Moses registered horrified recognition of her imposed identity. She pulled with scandalized strength, until the link between them snapped almost tangibly, and the flight deck vanished from her sight.

"Eisberg!" She flailed around wildly within her memories, seeking her unwanted teacher. "How dare you! How fucking *dare* you—"

She was back in the darkness, and without hesitation leaped back toward the world. But this time something caught at her as she moved, and pulled her along—at the same time as something else, incredibly strong, began to pull her in the opposite direction. Then other forces were seizing upon her, pulling her away from her hot, compact center. It was like her first, fumbling experiments in the blackness, but this time as if she had lost all control over her expansion, as if she were being deliberately drawn and diffused toward some ultimate dissolution in the eternal lightlessness. . . .

She fought, the only way she knew how. As hard as the forces drew her outward she willed herself to return to her center, to that distant, tenuous spark just barely perceptible within the widening sphere of her existence. She met each new pull head-on, pitting her will against their implacable traction, searching grimly for the strength that seemed the only defense against this new assault. The dark sought to wrench her asunder, to burst her like a fragile soap bubble, and she resisted, meeting each new attempt with the solidity of obdurate teak.

Slowly, she began to win.

The forces never lessened in their attack; there seemed to be no limit to the strength they could draw on. But she discovered that they were incapable of exhausting her either, that all their might could not compel her surrender and that her own strength slowly grew as she withdrew back toward her center.

She drew in closer to the flame of her resistance, closer than she had ever withdrawn before. The forces continued their grim assault and she could only continue to retreat in upon it, until suddenly the bright fire of her resistance was no longer within her: she was within it—

—and suddenly the darkness was something apart from her.

She was there, "in the flesh," if such a term made any sense under the circumstances. Where before she had existed in the darkness only as a disembodied sense of self, now she seemed to have an actual, physical presence: she could "look" down and "see" her body, or a representation of her body, evidently as solid and correctly assembled as the flesh she inhabited out in the real world.

Abruptly she was aware of a new sensation, of a continuity of her body, an awareness of linkages reaching out into the darkness around her, into the real world outside. It was as if she had reproduced herself in miniature at the heart of her being, with each atom of her inner self linked on some primal level to the grosser matter of brain and body beyond. It was as if she had forged a core of refined, compressed identity from the cruder materials within which she had struggled all her life. She looked out on the darkness, and it was as if her compressed existence granted her sight a clarity and penetration she had never noted before. She could *see* the stuff of the blackness, swirling and eddying like dense fog on a narrow street, and it parted to her desire, wafting aside from her gaze, letting her see ever more deeply...

...and then she saw Eisberg. The darkness parted around him as he walked—walked, as if there were something there to walk *on*—toward her. His smile this time held a genuine satisfaction, and an eagerness that immediately put her on guard.

"Congratulations," he said. "You've done it."

"Thank you," she said cautiously. "What have I done?"

"The concentration of identity," he announced. "The separation of the self from the clumsy support of crude neural processes and organic constraints is the single crucial step in the mastery of your talent. All else is mere trickery, technique, delusion. And now you've mastered it."

"I'm glad to hear that," she said. "Now what do I do with it?"

"You? Nothing, I'm afraid." The Eisberg nodality began

to walk toward her again, and Mitsuko was suddenly acutely conscious of the fact that her distilled identity included no perception of clothing. It was a ridiculous concern down on this level, and had it been anyone else but Eisberg she would have been able to ignore it. But it *was* Eisberg. "I'm afraid I haven't been entirely frank with you regarding our ambitions for yourself. But then, I didn't have much choice." The blackness swirled briefly around him. When it cleared, he was as naked as she was. "I wasn't built that way."

"No," she said. The fear was a streamer of cold lightning up her spine. If she had possessed breath to draw down on this level, it would have caught in her throat. "No. Oh, no."

"I'm sorry," he said, "but we really couldn't trust the elimination of our friend White to an uncontrolled outsider. And we could not write off the time and effort we invested in you before you left, or trust our privacy in your hands."

"Then why train me more?"

"As you were, you were of no use to us. We need more refined tools."

She tried to flee, but her new density failed her. The suddenly insubstantial blackness would not support her, offered her no footing for escape. Eisberg reached her easily, and his hands were like hot irons on her bare shoulders.

He turned her, the heat of his touch scoring her flesh, and then the fire was in her mouth as his lips covered hers. It spread, growing fiercer with each minute, incandescent, consuming. Where his skin touched hers their bodies melded, limbs fusing to limbs, face to face, breasts grafting to a slender, fashionably muscular chest as he took her in, absorbed her, reshaped her in his own corrupt image.

She screamed, with all the weight of her existence behind it, a single blind assertion of identity, and the scream was a cleaving blade that sundered them and threw them apart.

Mitsuko willed herself not to collapse, not to seek the beckoning oblivion of unconsciousness as the pain of the separation racked her and crumpled her into a huddled ball.

She straightened, slowly, stubbornly, against the agonized cramps and spasms that tried to pull her down again, and forced herself to seek out her assailant.

He stood some distance away, swaying uncertainly, eyes blank and confused, as if something had happened he had not been warned to expect. But he stood, and his very existence was an intolerable affront that Mitsuko Tamura would tolerate no longer.

She screamed again, but this time the scream was deliberate, an attack, with all the power of her pain and her anger and her new awareness of identity behind it, and it pierced Eisberg like a lance.

She expanded her awareness outward again, but this time Eisberg was trapped against it, driven out before it like a corrupt bubble of marsh gas driven to bursting by its own foulness.

"Not again!" Mitsuko screamed. "Never again!"

"You don't know what you're doing!" There was pain in Eisberg's voice, but it was a simple physical agony; it paled beside the suffering he had inflicted on her for so long, and she paid it no mind. "You mustn't do this!" he screamed, as he stretched thinner and wider across her expanding self. *"You can't do this!"*

"I can! I *can* do it, you bastard! You're *hollow,* there's nothing to you! And I'm going to prick your bubble!"

He protested again, but he was distorted now by the impossible volume of identity he was being forced to contain, and the sound of the scream was nothing intelligible, nothing like human—

—and he was gone, just like that, as a soap bubble is gone, as a picture vanishes from a screen when it is unplugged. Mitsuko Tamura was alone in her mind for the first time in days—and for the rest of her life, if she wished.

She found the real world without effort this time, slipping easily and instantly back into her body and her cabin. Her physical shell was unmarked by her struggle, but she bent to the tap and drank deeply of clean, filtered water, to drive the taste of Eisberg from her mouth, and washed with rough, scraping strokes to remove the stain of his touch from her.

Only then did she become aware of the pounding on her door, and that it had been going on since she returned.

She opened the door and Moses Callahan was through it in a rush, his hands gripping her arms with rough, frightened strength as he bulled her back into the cabin and up against the far bulkhead.

"*What have you done to me?*" he demanded, and she looked into his eyes and started to protest—

—and suddenly there was a second skein of memory in her mind, not Moses' but her own, yet not her own. It was as if all the time she had faced her final test against Eisberg she had also been bolting from the flight deck to rush blindly down the corridors of the *Wild Goose*, to stand hammering in helpless terror on the door to her cabin. . . .

Too late, she recognized Eisberg's last lesson to her.

"Moses, I'm sorry," she stammered. "I didn't mean to do it, I didn't want to, I wouldn't have—"

He didn't want to listen. He had found a physical target on which he could vent his anger and fright, and the right or wrong of the matter had become irrelevant to him.

"Be damned to you!" he raged. "You didn't *want* to! You were in my *head!*"

She could have stopped him; she could have compelled him to release her. She had the skill now, and the strength. But her dismay at what she had done to him already, however unknowingly, would not let her act.

"Moses, I'm sorry," she said again, forcing a calmness into her voice. "I would never have done what I did to you of my own choice. It was forced on me. But I'll never do it again."

"By God, you won't!" he shouted, drawing back a heavy fist that could have broken her head like a fragile vase. But she didn't flinch away or resist. She leaned against the wall and watched him, forcing herself to accept his anger.

It defeated him. He could have hit her had she resisted. He could have struck an opponent. But for all his rage, she did not present enough of a threat to him to let him throw the punch he had drawn back. Like an old wolf faced with a surrendering opponent, he was thwarted.

He released her and stepped back, the fist still half-cocked by his head as if he had no idea what to do with it now. Stiffly, he let the hand drop, and even without probing she could feel the iron restraint he laid over his anger, a restraint that surpassed anything she might ever have been capable of.

"I want you off my ship," he said, in cold, rough, controlled tones. "Whatever the hell happens at Avalon, I want you *gone*." And without waiting for her answer, he turned and left the cabin.

Mitsuko was left alone in the cabin, stunned by the violence of Moses' reaction, helpless in the face of his anger, the more so that it had come just as she thought she had fought her way to some measure of control over her own life. Now her first fleeting taste of freedom was soured by this new blow, struck from a direction from which she had never thought to be attacked.

Astonished, she saw that Moses was laying all his fright and misery, rolling down from the flight deck in an almost tangible wave, on her. The White nodality was eroding his crumbling will in a way he could not perceive, any more than a rock perceived the trickling rainwater that slowly wore away its substance. But he was aware of Mitsuko now, through her unknowing lapse, and he was making connections that were not there.

The monumental unfairness of it all was blinding, insufferable. All her own pain, all her enduring of the Eisberg nodality and the ugly memories it had raised, counted for nothing, because Moses was not aware of them. She could have erased his anger and mistrust as easily as flipping a switch—but she would not do that, because that would have been Eisberg's way, the way she had repudiated. Yet her forebearance did her no good at all, because it would never be recognized. Moses Callahan could broadcast his rage and frustration unawares throughout the ship, and she had to accept it, because he could not know she was vulnerable to it. It was not a willful act intended to cause her pain, to inflict himself upon her. But there was no way she could reply in kind, because she had the knowledge now to recognize what she would be doing. That was the difference between them, and it was the difference that bound her to inaction.

Moses' anger thundered back from the flight deck with the mesmerizing ominousness of distant surf heard through a fog. Down in their cabins, Luther Orange and Nullman slept. The little accountant lay immersed in his dreams, surrounded by bright fire and delusions of effectiveness. Luther Orange's dreams seemed quieter, but Mitsuko shied off from probing them too closely, for fear of the White avatar and a confrontation she still dreaded. The Eisberg nodality had claimed that its White counterpart was helpless without an aware consciousness to work through, but then she should never have trusted it in the first place, any more than she would have trusted its creator.

In all the ship there was only one place of quiet.

Hallorhan sat up in his berth as he keyed the door open and Mitsuko stalked into the cabin. She sat down heavily on the seat end of the berth, scowling blackly at the empty air in the middle of the room.

"Hello," Hallorhan said. "Can I do something for you?"

"No," she said shortly.

"Oh." He had been in bed but not sleeping; he had shed his coverall and undone the torso seal of his pressure slick. The dark garment melded with the shadows of the cubicle so that he watched her, a disembodied face framed by still hands, his expression unreadable.

The silence was there, beckoning. Mitsuko reached for it, sought refuge in it . . . but she had learned, too well.

Before, she had welcomed Deacon Hallorhan's silence as a shield against the imposition of the uncontrolled thoughts of others. But she had never experienced the silence itself, as the phenomenon it was, rather than as the absence of other input.

For the silence did have a substance of its own, and a texture perceptible to her new, finer senses.

There was something leaden about Hallorhan's silence, something inert, something not just lifeless but stone dead, as if whatever vitality it might once have possessed had been oppressively ground out of it. It felt rough to her new perceptions, calloused, as though once-healthy tissue had been deliberately burned and scarred. She remembered Eisberg's brief warning about Hallorhan's condition, and she found herself inclined to believe the deceitful nodality in this one matter. For Hallorhan's silence had about it the feeling of a crude and hastily erected defense, a desperate effort to keep something out—or in.

But it was the only silence she could find, and she went to it as she might have sought the roughest hovel in preference to enduring a torrential downpour. Nevertheless, it was another refuge spoiled for her, as the Institute and now the *Goose* had been spoiled, and it rankled.

"Goddamn it," she said sourly, unaware she had spoken aloud.

"Goddamn what?"

"What? Nothing," she replied, confused by his interruption.

"Oh, come on, now," Hallorhan said. "You didn't just come in here to curse a pronoun. What's the matter?"

"Nothing is the matter. Shit."

"I'm not going to get any sleep like this."

"You never sleep anyway."

"You never know, I might want to give it a try sometime."

"Well, don't let me stop you."

"Right. You'll sit there and watch me while I try to catnap between expletives. Look, this isn't the wardroom, Mitsuko."

"You want me to leave?"

"Unless you're here for a reason, yes, no offense."

"Then all right, I'll leave. What the hell, that makes it complete, doesn't it?"

"Makes what complete?"

"Moses is throwing me off the *Goose* when we reach Avalon." She fought down the hot, angry tears that had surprised her with their appearance. Actually saying it had given the event a reality she had been able to deny it before then.

For the first time since she'd met him, something had surprised Deacon Hallorhan. "What the hell for?"

For all her anger, the old fears drove her back from the whole truth. "I don't know. I guess he finally got tired of putting up with Spooky Tamura."

"That's ridiculous. He can't just do that."

"He's the captain and it's his ship. Of course he damn well can."

"Complain to Mission House. He can't just beach you without cause."

"How much cause does he need? If he's dissatisfied with me as crew, that's the end of it—his word against mine, and it's his ship. Besides, even if Mission House ordered me held to articles, what would it be like trying to work that way? No, forget it. If he wants me out, then I'm gone."

"I don't know what to say. I'm sorry—"

"For what? You don't know how it feels, you've never stayed with a ship for a whole run yet. I'm not leaving, I'm being thrown out—and I *hate it*."

"I know what that feels like," Hallorhan said quietly.

"Do you?"

"Sure. Do you think I wanted that discharge?"

"Then why'd you take it?"

"Well, like you said, what would it have been like if I'd stayed?"

"Damn right. Goddamned right. They can do it, can't they? They can want you, they can use you, they can make whatever they want out of you—but God help you if you ever want something back."

"That's the way it works," Hallorhan agreed. "The only thing you can hope for is that sooner or later you'll stop caring, one way or the other."

"One what way?"

"Either you decide you can live with what they want to make out of you, or you can decide you don't give a damn what they have in mind—whoever your 'they' is—and take your chances on going your own way."

"Yeah? Which did you choose?"

"Oh, me, well . . . I've been going along with their joke for quite a while now. I don't mind admitting it's getting a little old."

"So why the hell don't you take your own advice?"

"Don't think I haven't considered it. Just sometimes, it's a little harder than you'd think to let go, especially when you've had a lot of help in hanging on."

"I would love to let go. I'd love it. But I can't."

"Why not?"

"Well, the way they have me boxed in, letting go would be exactly what they want."

"Then don't let go."

"That hurts."

"I don't know what other choices there are," Hallorhan said. "At least those are the two I was given. Just what is it they want you to let go of?"

Mitsuko shook her head. "I can't explain it."

"Can't? Or won't?"

"What's the difference?"

"The difference is one you can do something about, the other you can't."

"It's that easy, is it? Won't, I guess."

"Then you're stuck."

"Thanks a lot."

"What do you want me to say? I can't make your decisions for you. But if it's that tough, then give it up, let them make your decisions for you. I don't see what other choice you've got."

"No, dammit. Neither do I."

They sat in awkward silence for some seconds. Finally Hallorhan spoke.

"You're welcome to stay here if you want. Just make sure you lock the door when you leave." Then he rolled onto his side, facing the back of the berth. It was all the privacy he could offer her, or as far as he could retreat. She could not tell which, and the doubt rankled her.

After a time Hallorhan's breathing grew slow and regular, and Mitsuko sat alone and awake in the cabin, picking at his scarred, abrasive silence as though picking at a scab on her knee.

Moses sat alone with his betrayal on the flight deck.

His anger had surprised even him. He had been ready to *hit* Spooky, an action he would once have equated with stepping on a kitten. Spooky Tamura was someone you tolerated good-naturedly, or were occasionally amused by, or sometimes felt a half-formed, unvoiced paternal protection for. But the thing about Spooky Tamura that he had come to value most clearly was that she was not a threat, that in a universe of powers at best indifferent, at worst inimical to the continued prosperity of Moses Callahan, there was one person he did not have to feel vulnerable to, or stay on his guard around.

But now all that had changed, drastically.

The Spooky Tamura he had found impossibly sharing his head was a harder creature all around than the Spooky Tamura he had thought he knew, all sharp angles and anger and grim assertiveness. But worst of all, he had felt inexpressibly certain that the Spooky in his mind didn't give a good goddamn about Moses Callahan, or about anything at all save herself and whatever her reasons were for being there.

It was hardly a new attitude to Moses. But he had never thought to equate it with harmless Spooky Tamura, or to find it expressed in such shocking intimacy. He had found something inside his head that did not care whether he lived or died, just as the rest of existence around him seemed not to care, and both the unexpected proximity of the offense and its unexpected source had combined to briefly overwhelm his strained defenses.

His rage shamed him; his loss of control embarrassed him. But he did not think of rescinding his dismissal of her. She had frightened him too badly for that, for him to cling to his old, glib impression of Spooky Tamura as a harmless eccentric to be indulged. When they reached Avalon, he would beach her.

But the decision left him more completely alone than he could remember ever having been before. . . .

# CHAPTER 11

James Emerson White reveled in the power his hands had brought him.

He looked up into the night sky of Avalon, to the stars from which came his freedom. The *Wild Goose* was still half a day out from planetfall, but his nodality had already reunited itself with him, rushing ahead of the ship at the speed of thought, bearing with it the familiar memory of nerve and aggression and control he never seemed to find quite so clearly otherwise. He often imagined that the nodalities he shaped represented the true, essential James Emerson White, freed of the nagging, weak fears and uncertainties that had been forced upon him for so many years before his revelatory discovery that those fears had simply been the feeble, hypocritical constraints of a world that feared ability it could not control. The nodalities had only purpose and power, and he treasured their existence as much for the sense of vicarious, unblinking mastery they gave him as for the wealth and power they brought back to him.

The thought of power and fear brought his gaze down to the horizon, where the vulgar glare of Balm banished the stars from the lower half of the sky.

The effrontery of it enraged him afresh every time he considered it. For what the villa had cost him, a decent view seemed little enough to ask, yet instead he was expected to tolerate this urban excrescence on his skyline. But it was what the city held and hid that stoked his anger so thoroughly, for somewhere in the maze of those gleaming streets the Institute Annex hid and plotted against him, tried to thwart and frustrate his every attempt to profit by

148

his natural gifts because of the threat they saw in him. They could not break him directly, for there was no one in their provincial little Annex who could match him for natural ability—but they were many and he was one man, a lion beset by jackals, driven from his rightful prey by yapping, cowardly numbers. The metaphor pleased him, almost as much as the knowledge that soon they would have to leave him be, once the trigger was in his hands. He would never use it, of course, for that would be wasteful in the extreme, trading a perfectly good city for freedom from the harassment of the Annex, but they could never be sure of that.

And actually the notion did have a certain dramatic appeal, to rid himself of his persecutors in a single fiery consummation. Wherever they hid in the city, in the brief instant left to them before they were blown to luminescent dust, the Annex would surely have to admit they were playing out of their league. And if it went wrong, he could always leave in his very own starship, crewed by willing nodalities, to seek his new fortunes in a universe ripe with unsuspecting potentials.

The ship, the ship. White could understand what drove Moses Callahan. The freedom it would give him, the ability to send his agents out to the very stars themselves, at will—even the idea of it thrilled him. Moses Callahan's fears, and the ease with which "he" had manipulated them, earned his total contempt: the man didn't deserve a ship. It was only right that someone who knew how to use it should take it from him. With Luther Orange to captain her and White to give him proper direction, the *Wild Goose* might very well be his ultimate tool.

And all that stood between him and it was half a day and three crippled people. Which was no obstruction at all. . . .

Moses crouched in the access hatch to the flight deck, meeting both their stares: Hallorhan's, its usual impassive mask; Mitsuko's, a mixture of anger and misery vying for ascendance. He felt a stab of regret once again for his decision, but he suppressed it ruthlessly, unwilling to trust it as being of his own creation.

"Haven't you got duties aft?" he demanded roughly. She

started to speak, then thought better of it, squeezing past him and off the bridge.

"What's going on with you two, Captain?" Hallorhan asked.

"Nothing that need concern you."

"Like hell. I'm aboard this rust-bucket, and she's in charge of keeping it in one piece, and if you're throwing her overboard I'd like to know why."

"Because it's the captain's privilege to select his crew," Moses snapped. "And because she isn't in charge of keeping this ship in one piece. That's the master's responsibility, just like every damned thing else on board, and I'm still the master here, much as people overlook that."

"I don't recall ever disputing the point."

"Well, that makes you one of a dwindling minority. The ship is mine," Moses said formally, calming down. "I relieve you."

Hallorhan leaned back from his boards. "The ship is yours."

Moses turned in his seat to watch the pilot climb out of his station. "We should be picking up Avalon Highside Approaches in about four hours," he said.

"Right."

"I want you back down here then, so get yourself some sleep now, while you can."

"Yes, sir."

"I mean that, Deacon. Go to bed."

"Sure, Captain." The pilot paused at the hatch. "How do we handle this when we touch down?"

"That trigger will never get through customs, will it?"

"Are you joking? It's still got its issue markings on it."

"So they must be planning on taking it off before we're boarded."

"Probably."

"Nullman's got his little gun back, you know."

"How did that happen?"

Moses sighed. "Orange came and got it."

"And you gave it to him?"

"Not really. He took it."

"And you let him?"

"You weren't there. You don't understand."

"Well, I guess I don't."

"It's not as if it matters," Moses said. "They'll have to return to their cabins for the landing anyway. We can bolt them in and just keep them there."

"Sure."

"Then when we touch down, we just stay buttoned up and yell for Fleet. That should work."

"I guess it should."

"Sure it will. Now you go turn in."

"Aye, aye, sir. See you later."

Mitsuko was waiting by his door when he returned to his cabin.

"Not much longer, is it?" she asked.

"Not really. We'll be taking an assigned course from Highside in about four hours. We should be down inport maybe a watch after that."

"So that's it, then. I guess I should go pack."

"It's going to take you twelve hours?"

Mitsuko laughed shortly. "Not likely. I've never been one for collecting things."

"No, me neither."

"You going ashore at Avalon?"

"Thought I might."

"I wouldn't be in any rush," she said. "This isn't a bad ship, on the whole."

"That's very tolerant of you."

"It's the truth."

"For God's sake, he just beached you!"

"He's scared, Deacon."

"What's he got to be scared of? You?"

"He thinks so. And I'm not sure he's wrong. But I'm probably the least of his problems, just the one he could do something about."

"He's got a hell of a way of solving his problems. Did you know he gave Nullman back his laser?"

"Yes."

"You do. And do you know why he gave it back?"

"I don't think he could help himself."

"Now what does that mean?"

"Deacon," Mitsuko began, as though uncertain what she should say—or how much. "There are things going on aboard this ship that you and Moses don't have the slightest idea about."

"Like what?"

"If I could tell you in any way that you'd believe me, I would. But—just get that trigger off-loaded, get Orange and Nullman off this ship, and get out of here again, as fast as you can. Lift out empty, if you have to."

"We can't go anywhere without an engineer."

"You'll be able to sign an engineer on easily enough. We're all over the place. But lift out of Avalon *fast*."

"What's going on here?"

"I can't—"

"And what have you got to do with it?"

"I can't answer that, either. It's something that's been following me for a long time, and it's something else none of us are to blame for. I'll do what I can to keep my end of it clear of you, but the longer you stay inport, the harder that will be."

"Callahan will never believe this. And I don't blame him."

"He has to believe it. You have to make him, Deacon."

"How? 'Hey, Captain, that flaky little engineer you beached told me to tell you to get offplanet by sundown, no matter what'? We're going to be mixed up with Fleet, we're going to be mixed up with customs; there's no way we'll be allowed to leave before they're finished with us. And even if we could, he won't believe any warning you give him. Beyond that, I don't think it would do any good, given the shape he's in."

"Then you'll have to take care of him."

"I don't understand you, I really don't—"

"He's not a bad man, Deacon."

"He's coming apart at the seams."

"Somebody wants him to. And there's nothing he can do about it. Do you remember how we talked about the way they can use you, make anything they want out of you? Well, they've been trying to bend Moses Callahan into shape for at least two years now, and he just hasn't got much left to fight back with."

"You've known about it for two years—"

"No, no, no. But that's how long they've been working

on him. He can't fight them anymore, and I'm not going to be here. That leaves you."

"And just what am I supposed to be able to do?"

"Come on, you're not going to tell me an ex-marine can't take care of himself."

"This one can't, even if I thought I had to. I told you I was too good a soldier for Fleet's taste, remember? Well, they didn't want to turn all that enthusiasm and talent out on the street without exercising a few options of their own."

"Oh." Suddenly Mitsuko understood. The silence, the scarring that had produced it, were a defense—but a defense turned inward, against the mind it sheltered. "You mean you can't even protect yourself?"

"Sure. I can run, real fast. Failing that, you could beat me to death with a feather-duster and I couldn't raise a hand to stop you."

"Even if you wanted to?"

"Oh, I'd want to, I promise. But I couldn't. The doctors were quite explicit on that point."

"How do you know—"

"They told me. They have ethics, you see—they can't go mucking around inside your head without telling you what they're doing. You can't stop them doing it, but you know why they're in there."

"But if they've cured you—"

"Who said anything about curing me? They just don't want me going and declaring my own wars. They don't give a damn if I think about it."

"Or talk about it."

"Talk is cheap. I don't think they're too worried about my talking anybody to death. But I sometimes wonder if the treatment took as completely as they wanted it to take. I think I can talk about it a little *too* easily."

"You just can't act on it."

"No. Not yet, anyway."

"Oh. Too bad."

"I can't say I think so."

"Literally." Mitsuko recoiled from an idea, born suddenly at the back of her mind and just as firmly refused. But the more she rejected it, the more solidly it returned....

"Well, warn the captain, please. Even if it won't do any good. I have to make the effort of asking."

"All right," Hallorhan said. "I'll do that."

"Thank you."

The cabin door closed behind him. Mitsuko stood there, her forehead pressed to the cool alloy bulkhead. The idea returned, so strongly that she probed inward angrily, looking for some sign that it had been foisted on her from outside. But she was alone within her mind, to the full limits of her perception. The idea was hers alone. The blame for it was hers alone.

She felt the door-track activate, vibrating faintly through the bulkhead. *No*, she thought urgently, *don't come back. Stay inside and maybe I won't*—too late. The door slid open and Hallorhan was there, looking down at her.

"Oh, God," she said, softly, despairingly.

"I thought you'd still be here."

"Why?" she asked. Hallorhan didn't realize she wasn't talking to him.

"Because you've been hanging around me for the last week. You look stupid standing out here; come inside."

She took her accustomed seat on the end of the berth. It left him with no choice but to stand. "You've never invited me in before," she said.

"That's not true."

"Yes, it—no, you're right, excuse me. But why did you invite me in this time?"

"Maybe the same reason."

Automatically, she probed into the silence, to no effect. She had never realized so strongly how much she had come to rely on her gift, however unconsciously.

"No," she hazarded. "No, I don't think so."

"Is that an opinion or an answer?" he asked, with a thin smile.

"Call it an opinion."

"All right."

"Then why?"

"I told you. I didn't want you standing around outside my door. It looks stupid. Besides, you seem to need to come in here, for whatever ungodly reason, and it doesn't do me any harm, so why not?"

"Thank you," she said, and the words curdled in her

mouth. "You're right. I do need to come in here. I need the quiet."

"You keep saying that. What quiet?"

"You. There's a quiet about you, Deacon. You don't impose on me the way other people do."

"There's a quiet around *me*?" Deacon laughed ruefully. "Lady, you ought to spend some time inside my head. Maybe you wouldn't want to talk about quiet then."

"Maybe I should." *There has to be another way to do this*, she thought desperately. But for her soul, she couldn't see it.

Hallorhan was scowling at her, puzzled. "If this is a come-on, it's the weirdest damned one I've come across."

*God* . . . "I'm sorry," she said. "I'm not very experienced at this."

"The way you're going at it, *nobody* is experienced."

"I guess not. I think I'd better just leave, before I make a bigger fool of myself."

He caught her lightly by the shoulder as she moved to the door. She flinched as though struck with a club.

"You're not making a fool of anybody," he said, and doomed himself.

Their teeth clashed as she reached up and kissed him quickly, clumsily. She recoiled, apologizing. "I said I wasn't very experienced at this—" but he'd already bent his face to hers a second time.

It was different this time, without Eisberg's distorting violence. Hallorhan was a slow, intent lover, patient with her awkwardness, her initial reluctances. Under other circumstances, she might have enjoyed it. But she had another reason for taking Deacon Hallorhan to bed. She needed time.

She withdrew into her mind, down to the solid, irreducible core of consciousness the Eisberg nodality had destroyed itself upon. Then she put her compacted, amplified senses out, seeking the scars of Hallorhan's silence.

It loomed up before her now like a weathered scarlet wall, seamed with myriad tiny gaps and fissures from past stresses laid upon it. Mitsuko moved forward and applied herself to the largest of the wounds, probing and digging. Although solid enough to the casual buffetings of daily life, the scar tissue of Hallorhan's conditioning crumbled like brittle pumice as she worked at it, widening the gap, deepening it, driving for the unseen substance of his mind behind it.

Somewhere in the real world above her, Hallorhan had eased them both into the narrow berth, careful not to let his greater weight discomfort her. Almost automatically, her slender body responded to the warmth of his wiry length against her, but down before the scar-wall the touch of him was only a distraction to be held aside, against the work she had to do.

The stuff of the wall was warm to her senses now, and translucent, like isinglass laid before a great fire. Something about the glow gave her pause, and she stopped her digging, suddenly uncertain. She had no right to do this, only need—but that was exactly the attitude she had rejected in Eisberg and the Institute. It was not her place to force Deacon Hallorhan against his will. But the peril he and Moses were in was in large part her responsibility, for it had befallen them through their knowing her, and she didn't know what else she could do—

—yes, she did. She would *not* use her gift to force Hallorhan into unwilling action. But she *would* break down the barriers of his conditioning, remove the inhibitions the doctors had laid down. She would give him back the choices they had denied him.

And that his choices would suit her ends perfectly would be just her good luck. Her hypocrisy appalled her, but it was the best she could do. She returned to the wall and assailed it again, ignoring the rising warmth and the increasing radiance behind it, ignoring her own self-disgust as she reached for the last obstructing layer of defense and struck it down.

The glare was blinding, a sun that seemed to fill the whole of her mind at once, brilliant and burning. She recoiled before it, fled back to the relative safety of her outer mind and the real world as Hallorhan gripped her with sudden, harsher strength. Even without her full presence her body had responded naturally to Hallorhan's caresses; still, she was not ready and it hurt when he entered her.

But that didn't explain her tears.

* * *

White was aware of the *Goose*'s impending landfall the instant Orange and Nullman were locked in their cabins. He acted swiftly.

Pylle arrived quickly in response to his unvoiced summons. Tall and muscular, clad severely and not a little pretentiously in the unrelieved black uniform that constituted his household's livery, Pylle headed up what James Emerson White liked to think of as his "irregulars," his coterie of hangers-on who fulfilled themselves on the reflection of his power, who shaped their identities in the image of his strength and served him loyally in exchange for their assured superiority over others less fortunate in their choice of master. In return, White welcomed their uncritical respect; it made a refreshing change from the troublesome self-assertion of the unthinking, unaware masses he thrived on.

"Captain Orange has returned with a new and interesting property, Pylle. I would like you to arrange to receive it without any bothersome formalities."

"None at all, sir?"

"None, Pylle."

"Yes, sir. Any suggestions?"

"Yes. The master of the ship Captain Orange has returned aboard, the *Wild Goose*, will be summoning official assistance immediately upon their arrival. I shall arrange it so that your services will be eagerly accepted instead."

"That will make it easier, sir."

"Of course. Assemble a detail, perhaps four men, and proceed to the spaceport. You will receive further guidance upon your arrival."

"Yes, sir. An armed party?"

"That might be most convenient, Pylle."

Pylle looked over the four men in the groundcar with satisfaction. Like himself, they were fit, hard, prepared for action, confident of their own abilities and the strength of their employer, whose presence within his mind Pylle sensed like a clear, stern eye overseeing his every action. They passed without challenge into the service zone of the spaceport, steering with a certainty beyond anything their own senses could have given them.

They found the customs van where they had known it

would be, the two customs agents and the Fleet Arm officers within slumped forward in their seats, the result of a simple manipulation of the sleep centers in what laughingly passed for their brains. Pylle leaned in through the open door and drew his laser, the cleanest weapon to hand for such a job, and assured the permanence of their repose. The uniforms fit well enough, and within minutes the van was on its way once more, to answer its urgent summons.

"Here they come," Moses said. The customs van was centered in his screen, floating swiftly toward the grounded ship. "We may get out of this yet."

"Looks that way," Hallorhan said. He seemed more alert than Moses had ever seen him, almost keen as he watched the approaching van. He looked over to Moses. "Do you need me here, Captain?"

"Well, they aren't here yet. Why?"

"I thought I'd go check on our passengers."

"I shouldn't think that would be necessary, Deacon. They're bottled up safely enough."

"Yes, sir."

"Don't go sounding all doubtful on me like that," Moses said. "Here, I'll call it up and you can see for yourself—oh, *hell*."

The terminal showed the shipboard security locks canceled throughout the length and breadth of the ship. And it said he had done it.

"It isn't possible—"

"Terminals don't lie, Captain," Hallorhan said. He was already out of his seat and reaching for the door-plate.

"But I *didn't*."

"Lock this behind me—" Hallorhan broke the command off short as the door opened and Nullman's laser preceded the little man into the flight deck.

"Nobody mo—" he began. But Hallorhan didn't wait to hear what instructions he was disobeying.

He was in an awkward position, his head on a level with Nullman's knees. But his right hand stabbed up, fingers locked together in a tapered spearpoint, driving into Nullman's groin and tearing down. Nullman screamed and doubled over, his laser pulse slashing through the padding of the pilot's station. As he folded over, Hallorhan raked the laser from his limp fingers with his left hand as his right drew back and lashed out again in a hooking punch that struck into the side of Nullman's head with a sound like two cinder blocks striking. The two blows pulled the crippled accountant down into the pilot's station. Moses stood just as Hallorhan's right hand rose and fell a final time, and by the time Moses had risen to where he could see into the pit Nullman was dead, a black bruise spreading over most of his temple.

Hallorhan never even broke stride, turning smoothly back to the door. "Lock this behind me," he repeated, "and don't let anyone in until I get back. That includes those customs boys."

Then he was out and gone, running easily down the corridor, with no footfalls to mark his passing.

Mitsuko powered down her engineering boards for the last time. The fans whined to a halt above her, the stabilizers in the heart of the ship slowed to a crawl, the massive fusion plant cooled to a housekeeping trickle of power. The familiar actions came too easily, were finished too fast—but then no pace would have been slow enough to suit her, for each task she completed brought her that much closer to a confrontation she dreaded—and to a beaching, even if she were successful.

She turned at the sudden sound of an opening hatch, knowing whom she would see before she had half-completed the motion.

Luther Orange stood in the opening, his bulk blocking her view of the corridor beyond. She reached out slowly, probing, and found that he was alone behind his eyes. Wherever James Emerson White was now, he was not pulling the strings of his avuncular puppet.

"The engine room's off limits to passengers, Captain," she said, watching him. "You should know that."

Chilled, she watched him move to the tool locker as her probing found the murder in his heart.

"Yes, I know." He rummaged about in the locker, and she felt his relief as he came up with the laser welder. He had been concerned that he might have to kill her directly, by hand, and thought to spare her any more pain that was unavoidable. His courtesy did not impress her.

"You're alone," she said, easing up from her chair, because he would expect it.

"No. Our friend Nullman is on his way to the flight deck—"

"I mean White's gone, Captain."

Luther Orange looked at her, surprised. "He said you had some ability . . ."

"Nobody's making you do this," she said, backing away, reading his intent to force her into the corner where she could not flee. He would have to get close with the welder, to compensate for its short-ranged collimation.

"Wrong. This is something I have to do. I'm going to have a ship, Miss Tamura. I've been promised, and I want it."

"So you'll kill us for the *Goose*?" Her anger drowned any sympathy she felt for his desperate yearning.

"I'll do whatever I have to. I did my damnedest to keep *my* ship by the law, but the law took her from me. So now I'll take this one. It's only justice."

"It doesn't seem very just to me."

The cold metal of the after bulkhead was a shock against her back.

"I can't help that," Luther Orange said. "I'm sorry."

He reached to turn up the power of the welder to the fullest—

—and she struck, lancing deeply into his mind, then expanding outward, in the manner in which she had destroyed the Eisberg nodality.

But this was no construct; it was a living, complete mind, with a depth and a complexity no nodality could ever equal. Her thrust was slowed, entangled, blunted by the thick weave of sentience around her.

Out of the midst of it, she suddenly sensed his resolution to fire, an instant's perception of willed action before it was lost in the confusion around her. She reached back along the links to her physical body in the real world and willed the strength from her legs. Her slight form collapsed awkwardly as the laser spattered metal from the bulkhead behind the space her throat had occupied a second before.

The mass of his living awareness was too thick to be expanded in the way she had destroyed Eisberg's avatar.

Instead she drove through it, deeper into his mind, down beneath his conscious thoughts, into and through the murk of his undervoice, whipped to such a frenzy that the dividing line between it and his consciousness had all but vanished, down into the unaware, automatic sendings of the self that mastered the most basic functions of the body that bore it. She reached out and enshrouded those primal commands, blocking them away as she might have blocked away the random noise of the streets in the old days. She reached out for the blackness in which she had suffered so greatly and learned so much, and wrapped the blackness around the inchoate node of Luther Orange's life. She was aware, distantly, of the heavy impact as his body dropped in his tracks. Through her own far-off eyes, she watched him fall; her corporeal nostrils wafted her the stink as he befouled himself. But she could only assume that her attack had caught the commands that summoned each fresh pulse of his heart, and so she held her block for long seconds more, until she was certain she contained only emptiness.

Then she withdrew, back to her own flesh, to look down impassively on the dead meat on the deck before her. It was difficult to connect it, somehow, with the murderous impulses of the man who had stalked her only moments before. Those were gone, destroyed, and behind them they left only a neutral, rotting husk.

She reached out into the rest of the ship, found Moses, alone and raging impotently on the flight deck; found Hallorhan, a brilliance impossible to observe for any length of time. She had succeeded with him, if she wished to call it success: the silence was gone forever. Instead he burned now with an intensity of life and alertness that bordered on the manic, and a driving, aggressive sense of self that brooked no contradiction. It was as effective a barrier to her probing as the scarred silence had ever been, but where the silence had been an obdurate and impenetrable barrier, like the cone of some ancient, dormant volcano, his new radiance was the fiery lava that burst forth now without restraint, overwhelming everything in its path. He was coming her way, she realized, and she tried her best to set up some sort of filters in her awareness, to cut down the most severely dazzling aspects of his brilliance. She had little success.

He stepped quickly into the engine room, half-turning as he did to look into his blind side. He swung back easily to face her, his gaze moving over Luther Orange's corpse in swift dismissal.

"Are you all right?" he asked.

Mitsuko nodded. "He was going to kill me," she said, with a shaking note in her voice she didn't have to fake at all.

"He didn't make it. This part of your old business? Or part of our current problem?"

"A little of both," she said. "They're hard to separate."

"No doubt." He bent and scooped up the laser welder from the corner it had rolled into. He studied it critically for a moment, then powered it down and set it back in the locker.

"We'd better get back to the flight deck. Those customs and Fleet people will be here any second."

Mitsuko swiftly reached out and probed the approaching van.

"They aren't customs men, Deacon."

"I know. They wouldn't be, or these two wouldn't have tried anything. Come on."

He turned and led the way up the corridor, pausing by his cabin door. "Just a minute." He stepped inside and emerged a moment later, carrying a worn crewpac. "Let's go."

They ducked back onto the flight deck, to see the customs van retreating back toward the service area.

"They just turned around and left," Moses said. "They didn't even try to signal us."

"They wouldn't have," Mitsuko said. "They knew it went wrong."

"And how did they know that?" Mitsuko could only shrug. "Don't put me off like that, goddamit—"

"It doesn't matter how they knew, Captain," Hallorhan said. "The thing is, they made their play and they blew it. Now we can call Fleet again, before they get reorganized."

"Yes, I suppose you're right."

"And then we decide what we're going to do about those bastards."

"I don't intend to do anything about them at all," Moses said, "except get out of their way and stay out of their way."

"That's too bad," Deacon said, opening the crewpac. The heavy silver thermal-charge pistol he drew out fit his hand as if it had grown there.

He wasn't afraid.

There was nothing in the world James Emerson White had to be afraid of; he had learned that years ago, when he had learned that fear was a chain too feeble to bind him, held as it was in others' hands, whose actions he could rule. But the sudden and irresistible severance of his link with Luther Orange, and his inability to reestablish it, had been a disconcerting shock, and he had sensibly withdrawn to reconsider the situation.

It had to have been the woman. Neither Callahan nor the pilot had shown any vestige of the talent within his nodality's ken—but neither had *she* shown the strength it must have taken to break his mental connections so readily. It was a puzzle; he knew how many years, how much pain it had taken him to master his gift. He refused to believe that she could progress so quickly, so suddenly. It was not a possibility, not for him and therefore not for her.

The Bethe trigger was lost to him, he had to accept that. And his only chance at taking the *Wild Goose* had vanished with Luther Orange, as, indeed, had his use for it. A ship without a captain was worthless to him. . . .

He stopped himself, and cursed his own timidity. A ship without a captain was useless to him. But there was still a captain available. He would show them all yet. He was not in the habit of being thwarted and did not plan to grow accustomed to it at this late date. . . .

The Fleet officers arrived in force this time, and authentically, in a combat sled with a supporting security element that ringed in the *Wild Goose* and turned back the port authorities without explanation. They took Moses much more seriously this time, with the weight of two dead Fleet officers to lend credence to his claim that he had a contraband Bethe trigger in his holds. And for all their anger over the deaths of their comrades, they were profes-

sional enough to establish that the crew of the *Wild Goose*
could not have been off committing a multiple homicide in
the service area while fighting off a hijacking attempt on
board their own ship. Moses had to wonder, though,
whether the Customs agents and Port police cooling their
heels outside the Fleet perimeter would be so tolerant
when they were finally granted their shot at him.

He needn't have worried. Fleet Arm wasn't about to let
an investigation of a major security breach be cluttered up
with scurrying local cops. The *Wild Goose* was processed
in through Fleet channels, her remaining cargo inspected
in finest detail, and her every memory bank and hidey-
hole gone through with microscopic thoroughness, until
even the most peregrinatory inquisitor would have been
bound to admit that if there were any commodity aboard
the *Goose* they hadn't been told about, hiding it in the
fusion plant had probably eliminated most of the evidence.

The only thing they did not find was the truth, and
Mitsuko saw no reason to enlighten them. There had been
a moment's curiosity when Moses had announced she was
leaving the ship there in Balm, but nothing in the law said
captains couldn't discharge crew. Moses, of course, did not
appraise them of the cause of her beaching: the victim of a
secret telepath has almost as much to lose by the revelation as his victimizer, if the claim goes unproven. No one
particularly wants to be branded a paranoid madman.

So pilot, captain, and engineer were left alone on the
tramp freighter once again, although none of them doubted
that they didn't want for reticent observers. The trigger
was carefully recrated and removed under heavy escort.

"That's it, then," Moses said, after the last stern-faced
officer (they must all have practiced that expression) had
gone. "It's finished, except for the one thing." He looked
at Mitsuko, waiting.

"You're making a mistake, Captain."

"This doesn't concern you, Mr. Hallorhan. You don't
know the way of the thing, so please don't interfere."

"He's right, Deacon," Mitsuko said. "I can't argue with
him."

"About what?"

"I did something I had no business doing. I didn't mean
to, but that doesn't change the fact that I did it. There's no

excuse." The brilliant radiance of his mania was a painful thing that reminded her continuously of her further, unvoiced guilt. Caught between his light and Moses' pain, she wanted to run, just as she'd run in the old days.

"You can't just throw her out, Captain."

"Why not?"

"Because, dammit, this thing isn't finished yet. All right, we're rid of the trigger, but do you think that's the end of it? It's not finished until we find these bastards, or sure as I'm saying it, they'll come and find us."

"We've nothing they want."

"We got in their way, Captain. Whatever else, they'll want payback. Face it, anybody who'd want a Bethe trigger can probably hold one hell of a grudge. So until we're rid of them, this thing isn't over, not nearly."

"Maybe when she's off my ship, it'll be over!"

"Like hell. She's the one who took out Orange, remember? While you were sitting up here twiddling your overage thumbs."

"That's right. They found Orange dead, with not a mark on him." Moses looked over to Mitsuko. "They thought that was very curious too, you know."

"I'm sure they did," Mitsuko said. "Thank you, Deacon, but forget it. I'm going, Moses. I'll go down to Mission House and post my availability, and then I'll be back for my things."

"You can take them right now."

"Then you can just throw them out the damned hatch. I'm not going to walk into Mariner's Hall looking like some damned vagabond! I'll be back later." And she was gone.

Hallorhan shook his head. "Dumb move, Captain."

"And none of your business, Mister Hallorhan, like I told you."

"That's where you're wrong, Captain. It's my business who I work for. You know, I was thinking I might threaten to walk myself if you beached her."

"Then why didn't you, if you felt so strongly about it?"

"Because I don't feel that strongly about it, Captain. She defended you to me, even after you beached her. But I can't see any future piloting for an hysterical lunatic like you, sir. So, if you'll excuse me, I think I'll just see her over to Mission House and try to line myself up a new berth."

And then he was gone, leaving Moses alone on the bridge with his fear and his guilt . . . and that was where James Emerson White found him.

Following the port cop's directions to Balm's Mission House, Mitsuko spent most of the long walk trying to figure out how many men were following her.

Three, she decided, who rotated the immediate tail on her, sound tactics on the busy street, against anybody but a telepath. To her, it didn't matter if they were six blocks away on the far side of a building, their concentration on her was as clear as an orbital beacon. She walked on down the broad, open avenue lined with low, elegantly curved white buildings, through the tall, fair crowds unaware of the hunt in progress in their midst. But her concentration on the three Fleet agents blinded Mitsuko to the presence of other watchers. . . .

Suddenly the Fleet agent nearest her was gone from her mind, blanked out with an unremarkable simplicity that almost went unnoticed for too long a moment. Then she recognized his disappearance, and reached out to search for the other two followers.

She found only silence. Alarmed, she reached out in all directions, enduring the sudden swell of crowd noise in her search for comprehension. She found nothing within a one-block radius, two blocks, three—

Without warning she felt an abrupt flare of attention on her, as if someone had struck a match inches from her face while she searched for a light miles away. She turned, and he was there. Pylle looked down at her from his greater height, and she realized that she had not noticed him because he had not been looking for her. His attention had been focused elsewhere, and only now was he truly seeing her, with the interest of fresh discovery. Someone or something had guided him to her.

She knew she was looking at the first of White's agents.

He had her by the arm now, in a grip both painfully tight and directed upward, so that she was half-lifted off her feet and borne through an open doorway nearby. They jostled their way past several passersby, none of whom protested. Mitsuko was astonished by their indifference, until she realized that it was not a lassitude of their own making. The people around her would become precisely as alarmed as White allowed them to become.

The door opened onto a small, high-walled garden. Pylle shoved her roughly through and followed, slamming the door behind her. Mitsuko turned to face him and read the murder in his eyes without needing to probe deeper. Without waiting, she acted.

As Luther Orange had died, she killed him. As Luther Orange had fallen, so Pylle fell, his desperate impulses for life walled off from the vital functions they governed. The sharp smell of ordure rose to clash with the perfume of the flowers.

And unlike Luther Orange, Pylle still stood. Clumsily, as though the familiar action had become a half-forgotten thing, mastered by a puppeteer working an unfamiliar puppet with warped sticks and frayed strings, he stood. And when he grinned at her, it was the contemptuous grin White had grinned at her that first day on the ship.

She recoiled in horror. Pylle was still unconscious; she had no sense of his awareness upon her now. And he should have been dead, even the autonomic processes of the body violently shut down by Mitsuko's attack. But he looked at her through eyes that saw, and stumbled toward her on legs that moved, and a pulse throbbed visibly in his neck.

She realized then what was happening. White was somehow animating his servant from a distance, providing his own vital spark to replace the one Mitsuko had snuffed out.

She retreated. She had no idea how to react to this ploy. Telepathically assaulting Pylle again would be useless; there was nothing there to attack. And to assault White himself she would first have to find him; she doubted he would give her the chance.

She turned to run—and a rough hand was clapped over her mouth and nose, she was thrown roughly against the wall, fighting for a breath that would not come, all skills forgotten in her blind, suffocating need for air she could not have—

—in her mind, the world flared brightly around her.

The hand was torn from her face as roughly as it had appended itself there, its black-clad owner pulled bodily off the ground as Hallorhan drew him back, both hands wrapped around his head from behind. Hallorhan kicked his legs out behind himself, throwing his weight straight back. The irregular was pulled over backward, his chin thrusting into his chest with impossible force. The sound of his neck breaking was lost in the impact of the two bodies on the tiled ground.

Hallorhan rolled clear of the body as more black-clad figures scrambled over walls and out of gates. They converged on him as one, but he was never there to be overwhelmed by their attacks. He would wait until they were committed to their charge, then step easily to one side or the other, and those terrible hands would fall on one of the irregulars, breaking, gouging, jabbing with practiced, unconscious ease. At first they would try to check their charge and turn to meet him. That only gave one of them the chance to reach him quicker, to die sooner. Finally they charged only in hopes of bulling past him, but he positioned himself between them and whatever egress they sought, and there was no passing him. Then they simply ran, seeking a safety they could not find, because the same walls that offered them concealment from the street now barred their escape. And Hallorhan moved after them, his hands like spears, like clubs, like knives, striking down the ones closest to the doors or the ones who turned to make a despairing stand, until he stood alone in the garden, its ruined flowerbeds host to a more grisly exhibition.

Then Pylle closed with him, grappling with a careless strength, for the mind that directed that body was not its own, and cared little for whatever harm might be done it. Those clumsy hands sought Hallorhan's throat and he struck them aside, striking at wrists, elbows, collarbones. But the pain Pylle felt was not White's pain, and he directed the body of his henchman in again and again, flailing at Hallorhan with ruined arms, seeking to bear him down beneath sheer lurching bulk. Hallorhan ignored the arms that struck at him, ineffectively now, for an arm with no bones left was a useless weapon. He struck to the body twice, driving the irregular back through the sheer impact, and then when he had the room he kicked out and Pylle fell, toppling off knees that could no longer support him.

White's raging stare looked out on him an instant longer, to be replaced by something very much like surprise. Then the animation faded from Pylle's features and his head lolled back, and there was no further movement in the garden, no sound save Hallorhan fighting for breath.

Finally he turned to look at Mitsuko, eyes bright with the light of his battle-lust, burning her with the knowledge of what she had unleashed.

"You're a hard lady to find," he said.

"I don't mean to be," she said. "I just seem to get caught up in things sometimes."

"Don't we all."

"What are you doing here?"

"This is the way they showed me to Mission House," he said. "I've got to stop in and post my availability."

"You're beached?"

"I beached myself."

"You shouldn't have done that."

"I thought I should. And no sense waiting."

"He doesn't deserve this."

"You didn't deserve this, either. I don't see what deserving has to do with anything."

"This is different. This is something I have to deal with."

"How?"

"These people were sent."

"I sent 'em back," he said cheerfully.

"I saw. That was—something." She moved among the bodies, aghast at the damage he had inflicted. "Are any of them still alive?"

"Sure. This one." Hallorhan looked up from the huddled Pylle.

"No, he isn't. Not that one."

"He's breathing."

Mitsuko drew nearer. Hallorhan was right; even bereft of White's guidance, Pylle's chest rose and fell in a ragged rhythm. The unconscious vital pulses were prodigiously strong, and she had not had the chance to suppress them as long as she had Luther Orange's. With the respite of White's intervention, Pylle would live. With the savagery of Hallorhan's attack, he would probably be crippled for life.

Mitsuko reached down cautiously into his unconscious mind. The Eisberg nodality had claimed that could not be done, but she was already learning that a living awareness had capabilities beyond those of any construct. She probed, and she searched, and in the end she found the information she wanted.

"Now what will you do?" Hallorhan asked.

"Now? I'll go meet the person who sent them."

"You can find him, of course."

"Yes."

"I thought you could." He grinned at her artlessly, happily. "I don't know what you are, lady, but you're really something."

"Whatever I am, you might wish I wasn't."

"Why? Because you opened me up? I'm not stupid," he said, at her look. "I knew something had changed for me. The only thing that could have done it was you. I'm obliged."

"You are?"

"Hell, yes. I was a good little boy because I had to be, lady. Now it's up to me. So where do we go next?"

"We don't go anyplace. This isn't your sort of fight."

"If some more of these losers come down on you, it won't be yours, either. It seems like it's my choice."

"Yes," Mitsuko said. "Yes, it is."

"Fine. So let's go back to the ship and let me pick up my thermal, and then we'll go see a man about a trigger."

The hatch of the *Wild Goose* was open when they got there. Hallorhan had hesitated, looking to Mitsuko, then turned and ducked swiftly into the ship when she nodded. She moved in behind him, slower, aware of what he would find beforehand.

"There's nobody aboard." He met her in the port corridor, bag in hand.

"I know."

"I thought you would. And the ship's hauler is gone. Any idea where he went?"

"Yes. Dammit, yes."

\* \* \*

He was under siege and he did not like it.

James Emerson White stood on the veranda of his villa, overlooking the night lights of Balm on the horizon. His senses swept the grounds of his estate with practiced ease, noting the placement of his remaining irregulars, fixing their locations and the muttering of their awarenesses firmly in his mind. He had no faith in their individual ability to deal with whatever had claimed Pylle and his team, but they would serve to warn him of its arrival.

The memory of it was dauntingly vivid in his mind, a brilliant, simplified distillation of self as strong in its way, perhaps, as he was in his. He had struck at it through Pylle even as it fell upon his men, but it had not even registered the attack, as though unwilling to consider its own vulnerability. But no matter. It would have to come to him, here, on his own ground this time, and on his own ground nothing challenged him.

He turned and paced back into the room behind him, where Moses Callahan slumped on a divan, staring morosely at an untouched glass.

"I'll give you credit where it's due, Captain," White said. "You and yours have caused me considerable grief. Luther Orange was a valued servant. Pylle and his men were loyal retainers. And I could have put that Bethe trigger to very good use indeed."

"Sure you could, now," Moses said, almost indifferently. "People like you are absolute demons for the using of things."

"That's the way the world works, Captain. Another way the world works is that when you take something, you pay for it. You've denied me the trigger, Captain Orange, and you've cost me several good men. I feel some kind of compensation is in order."

"You would."

"I do. And what would you suggest is fair compensation, Captain?"

"You tell me."

"You've denied me resources and cost me manpower. I think you should offer to replace them with like goods."

"I haven't got a trigger. And I've got no men."

"You do yourself an injustice, Captain. You have yourself. And you have your ship."

That roused Moses. "No. Not me. And not the *Goose*."

"I don't think you're in any position to refuse, Captain.
You owe me, and I mean to collect."

"You go to hell."

"Please."

"You goddamned monster—"

"Captain, I've heard this all before. Believe it or not,
you're not the first person ever to incur an obligation to
me. Now, you're here because I wanted you here, and we
can both agree that your feelings in that matter were fairly
irrelevant, can't we? Of course we can. And I'm sure you'll
accept that if I wanted you to *sell* me the *Goose*, you
would do so, on whatever terms I deemed appropriate,
wouldn't you?" Moses just glared at him. "It's the funda-
mental nature of our relationship, you might say. You have
something I want, and you give it to me."

He turned, and paced theatrically. "But—there is an
aspect of this not unfavorable to yourself. I think we can
both agree that I have a ship, Captain Callahan—but that
ship needs a master. You could be that master, Moses. You
could keep your ship, yes, that interests you, doesn't it,
and all you have to do is agree to take my service. It seems
a little thing more to give, when you can gain so much
more back by it, doesn't it?"

"I could keep the *Goose*?"

"On my terms. But yes, you would keep the *Goose*."

It was too easy, and he had been fighting scared too
long.

"Then I accept. What do I have to do?"

"Nothing Luther Orange couldn't handle, Captain, so
I'm certain you'll find it within your powers. Simply accept
my guidance as it's offered—"

White reached out, probing for Moses' mind, preparing
the avatar of himself that would bind the old captain to
him inescapably—

—and he was blocked.

Moses stared, as startled as the rogue telepath. He had
not seen Mitsuko enter, but she stood there as solid as his
shame, barring White from him.

"You leave him the hell alone," she said.

"How dare you—"

"If you want to meet something that's a threat to you,

you come after me, you bastard. I'm the one you have to fear, and you can't bend me like you've bent him."

"You can't threaten me!"

"Of course I can. I just did. But the threats are just starting." She turned to look at Moses. "I'm sorry about this, Captain. You should never have had to go through this shit. But he won't touch you now." Then she was gone.

Outside, the lawn was lit by a sudden burst of flame as a like fire burst in James Emerson White's head. A split second later, the report of the thermal charge detonating cracked through the room.

White whirled back toward the open patio, to see the gardens beyond his villa erupt in gunfire. Bright laser pulses stabbed between the trees and shrubberies, and the air crackled with the passage of high-velocity slivers.

Then there was a flash of actinic brilliance again, as the thermal charge pistol in Hallorhan's hand flashed a second time. There was another eruption of fire, and the explosion this time drowned out a brief human shriek. Suddenly the open room seemed terribly exposed and vulnerable.

Hallorhan moved easily through the ample concealment of the garden. His right hand was covered now with a silvered half-gauntlet, wired into the long unused terminals in his wrist. The lead that ran up his arm to the harness of the enerpac fed power to the pistol which rendered it as pure heat, and the old autofire circuits grafted into his arm were vibrant and alive again, in a way that made the rest of his body seem like half-animate clay to him.

Mitsuko followed him through the greenery, her senses reaching out, seeking their opponents, anticipating their murderous intent. She slapped Hallorhan's shoulder and pointed, and he whirled and fired in the same motion. Fire burst from the bole of a tree; a man screamed and fled for the safety of the shadows.

"Can you manage out here?" she asked him.

He just looked at her, laughing silently. She nodded and dropped to her knees, crawled away into the night.

Hallorhan turned, the weapon tracking with his eyes. A laser pulsed, firing blindly. His arm straightened and flame traced the light back to its source. No further shots came.

He dropped and rolled, the old habit, abandoning his revealed position. Fire chopped the bushes that had hidden him into salad. Then he was up and running toward the house, the weapon tracking from side to side, firing at the scattered men who engaged him in return. They were deployed badly and they were terrible shots. Amateurs, he thought disgustedly. It was hardly worth the trip.

The narrow side door to the house burned and shattered as he fired through it, somersaulting behind the shot. People screamed and scattered; he fetched up against the body of a woman, a servant—what was left of one, charred nearly in two by his entering burst. A man in black came rushing through the doorway, trying to bring a sliver rifle to bear as he entered. He never made it. Hallorhan moved through the door the man had used, and stalked off through the building.

Moses stood awkwardly in the middle of the empty room, confused and frightened. The firing had moved from the yard to the house itself, and White had abandoned him there, without even Mitsuko's shade for companionship. Things were happening, once more utterly out of his control but affecting him nonetheless, and for all his reluctance he knew he could not simply stand there and wait to be acted on once again.

He started for the door White had fled out of. But before he got there it opened, admitting one of White's black-clad goons. The man clearly had not expected to see Moses there—and he certainly never expected the heavy ashtray that Moses shattered along the side of his head. The man dropped, his shattered cheekbone a bloody ruin. Moses bent and relieved him of his weapon, a short-barreled sliver pistol, and moved on out into the hall. He had no idea what he would do with the gun, but he was sure he'd think of something.

The central atrium of the villa was dark and appeared to be deserted. Hallorhan didn't believe it for a moment. But it was the only way to go from the corridor other than back, and he knew there was nothing back behind him he wanted.

He studied the wall across from him, with its thick

columns supporting an interior tiled roof. Ideal cover. He lunged through the door and threw himself violently to the left, rolling for the cover—

—that was not there, as he rolled uselessly before a bare wall, and every gun in the household opened up on him from the arches across the way.

He made it back to his feet, firing into the shadows beneath the arches, lighting them up in brilliant silhouette. The fire from across the way dwindled, cowed by his attack, and he started to run—

—when the sliver caught him high in the side and spun him around against the wall, astonished at the amount of blood such a small wound could bring forth.

At the sight of his injury, his attackers opened fire with renewed vigor. He tried to get moving again but it was too late. There was no cover anyway, no place to run to. A laser pulse scored him through the ribs. A near miss blew fragments of sliver and masonry into his face. Another sliver drove a white-hot spike through his knee and the leg went out from under him, dropping him heavily to the ground. The world swam redly before his eyes at the impact; he was aware of other wounds, but far away, as if they had happened to another person. He wondered why his hand felt so light, why he missed the comforting weight of his pistol. . . .

He was not fleeing. James Emerson White fled from nothing. But there was little he could contribute to the defense of his property where he was, he told himself; it would be better if he withdrew to some place more central, more secure, from which he could rally his scattered forces and crush this inadequate threat once and for all.

But it was too late.

She stood there in the doorway, seemingly frailer than ever in the loose liberty jac, a stray, rebellious wisp of hair escaping beneath the rim of her cap. Her hands were jammed in her pockets as though against a bitter cold and her shoulders were bowed as though weighed down by the burden of this confrontation. But her eyes were wide and dark in her fine-boned face, and bright with all the anger and outrage that held her in his path.

"Oh, good," she said, and the scorn washed over him like an acid rain. "I thought you weren't coming."

"Bitch!" White screamed, and attacked, gathering up his strength and hurling in forward in one great smothering wave—

—and then *she* screamed, and the scream was an attack in itself that pierced him through and deflated him in mid-assault, to leave him floundering and confused.

"You'll have to do better than that," she told him. "I've had a very thorough education on account of you, Mister. Now it's time to pass out."

But he had gathered himself and attacked again in mid-thought, and it was all she could do to meet him and check his rush. It was like being down in the darkness again, in the flood and the hooks that had sought to pull her apart all at once, but this time the flood was aware of her, this time the hooks were being directed deliberately and with care, for maximum pull and effect. She fought back, tearing each hook free as it bit, forcing herself upright and stable in the torrent, but she saw no place to attack in her turn. All was black murk, roiling undervoice, fears and lusts and hatreds made real and grown strong. It was a solid wall of assault through which she could not break, try as she would.

Slowly she found herself losing ground, as though whatever base beneath herself she had created was being eroded away, as if all the pulling, clawing hooks were slowly toppling her backward, off-balance. She fought upright again, shrugged off the tearing hooks, but the current was still strong and for every hook she shrugged off three more sought her anew. Then, somewhere off in some unimaginable distance, a light went out, snuffed, and James Emerson White shrieked with gratification and pressed down on her with overwhelming power, bearing her back and down, into the limitless darkness.

He lay there, and the taste of his own blood was a bitter coppery warmth in his mouth. The pain in his leg had become a faded thing, as had the several uncountable hurts harder to locate in his body. That meant he was going into shock, he remembered, as did the increasing waves of cold running through him one after the other.

Treat for shock. Remember what they told you. Keep me warm. Elevate my feet. Come on, dammit. What was keeping them?

He could see them coming closer, the several men moving out of the cover of the columns. A metallic surface reflected a glint of starlight to the corner of his eye; his gun arm twitched unnoticeably as he moved his gaze and saw his pistol lying in the blood by his belly. So much blood. Where had it all come from? Control the bleeding first, no, breathing first, that was okay he was still breathing control the blooding the bleeding direct pressure tourniquets mean amputation don't tie it off unless you're ready to lose it done—

The men were coming closer and now he could see that they carried guns and wore black suits of some kind, not proper battle dress. Not ours. Not part of the mission. *Fuck'emall*—

He flipped onto his belly in one violent spasm. His gun hand followed his eyes to his weapon and came up firing, the blood boiling away from the emissions bell as he fired and the men in black fired and he bled and they burned—

She had been reduced to her irreducible core self, an unbreakable knot of identity deep within the darkness of her mind. White roared around her like a mighty gale, but she fought back with all her strength and he swept around her without effect now. But her ties with her outer body, with the real world, lacked her indomitable substance. She could feel them thinning out, being pinched off, blocked. Was this what she had done to Luther Orange, to the man in the garden? Was this how it felt to be killed within your own mind?

Suddenly the distant light flared up brightly again, only for a moment—but its reappearance brought a howl of anguish and anger from somewhere out beyond the torrent, a cry of primal frustration and vulnerability. Mitsuko leaped for it, the one weakness she could find in a universe of overwhelming power.

The flood tore at her, the hooks lashed out and bit. But she forced her way with desperate, fearful strength against the flood; took the hooks and drew them behind her until

they parted under the strain of her forever increasing
impetus; forced her way onward—

—and she was out, through, into the normal, vulnerable
weave of James Emerson White's mind. Without pause
she struck as she knew she had to strike, cutting through
the webs of thought and memory, ever deeper and further
into the vulnerable reaches of his self.

Snatches of memory and awareness yielded before her
as she brushed through them. A snippet of resentment,
*mommy has the money I know she does she does she does;*
a fragment of envy, *grades so damned easy he never
studies I won't either;* unformed lust, *sunlight through her
blouse see breasts almost see her nipples;* she recognized
all of them—in one way or another she knew them for her
own. The difference between Mitsuko Tamura and James
Emerson White was a thin one, if it existed at all, if it
existed for anyone. . . .

But she had not set out to prey on helpless people, as
White had, and Eisberg. She had not chosen to treat them
as things, creatures to be used and then discarded, shaped
to her own fleeting needs. And she would have left them
all alone for the rest of her life if she had been given the
choice. But they hadn't given her a choice; they had
badgered her, hounded her, tormented the people around
her to drive her in the direction they wished her to
go—and White was the one living embodiment of them all
that she could reach.

Destroy him and it was finished, or as nearly finished as
it would ever be. And that was all she needed to know.

She reached down and seized upon the primal impulses,
throttling them, choking them off. She met resistance,
more than any she had ever known, perhaps even as much
as she herself had. But she would not be denied. She
brought down the darkness, compressing it and forcing it
inward as she had once been compressed and forced, to
shape something that could not be altered further. The
darkness grew ever denser as she bore down upon it with
all her might, the primal impulses weaker and more
distant—

—and then it was done.

It seemed to take her forever to find her way back to her
own mind, as if White's attack had almost succeeded in

wiping away the links between herself and her own body. But finally she made it, to sit up infinitely weary and face his huddled corpse scant yards away. Her mental tiredness seemed to translate into physical exhaustion with the greatest of ease; it was all she could do to sit back against the cool corridor wall and revel in the blessed silence.

They froze facing each other, almost comically. The man in black had come out one door into the atrium as Moses had burst in through another, and now each confronted the other, weapons in hand.

The pistol in his fist seemed a ridiculously insubstantial thing to Moses as he half-raised it without thinking and fired. The man in black flinched and seemed to gape in astonishment as a bright red flower opened up on his belly, but he did not fall and he did not drop his gun, so Moses fired again, and again and again and again, until finally the man in black collapsed, still staring, his weapon unfired.

The atrium was littered with bodies, charred corpses in the middle of the tiled floor, and one lone figure sprawled prone at the base of a sliver-pocked wall, a gleaming silver pistol encrusted in dried blood clutched in his extended right hand.

Moses started toward him. "Deacon? Deacon, it's me, Callahan."

The bloody head turned, stiffly, with infinite slowness. The gun arm began to turn toward him along with it and Moses hesitated, but the pistol slid from nerveless fingers as the arm moved.

Hallorhan managed a blood-drooling grin. "Hey, Captain . . . you finally picked a side." He made a short grunting noise that it took Moses a moment to recognize as laughter. His gun arm began to move again; he made a child's pistol with his thumb and index finger. "Bang-bang, huh?"

"Whatever you say. Can you sit up?"

"What the hell . . . it can't hurt. . . ." Again the laughter.

Moses knelt and struggled to lift Hallorhan and prop him against the wall. It was like moving a dead weight. There was little life left in him.

"My God," Moses said softly. "What have they done to you?"

"They didn't do nothing, Captain. . . . I did it to my-

self. . . . Lady gave me a choice and I chose to come
along. . . ."

"Damn her—"

"Glad I did it, too, Captain. . . . no, mean it. All that
time they made me one thing, then they made me something else, whatever they wanted. . . . she took me some
way, let me be whatever I wanted to be. . . . and here I
am. . . ." The grunting laugh broke off short this time, in a
red, spumy cough. "Thank her for me, will you . . . ?"

"You'll thank her yourself," Moses said. Hallorhan laughed
again, the coughing coming sooner, and worse. "We're
going to get you out of here now." He pulled Hallorhan
forward, getting him over his shoulder, rising . . .

He wouldn't have thought a man could go any more
limp than Hallorhan had been. But he did, with a soft
liquid sigh and a sudden feeling of moist warmth down
Moses' back. Moses knelt again and eased Hallorhan carefully onto his back. His right arm moved stiffly to follow
the track of his sightless eyes, the autofire circuitry following its programming into the grave, pointing straight up
toward the ceiling. Moses gently turned the dead man's
head to the side and the arm lowered, to lay against the
floor with some minimal dignity.

Then, because there was nothing else he could do, he
turned and bolted from the atrium.

He thought they were both dead.

One of them had died for sure; the stink was unmistakable, and almost as bad in the narrow corridor as it had
been in the atrium. But at least nothing had burned in
here.

Mitsuko was staring at the body of James Emerson
White as Moses approached, her eyes wide, unblinking
black pools. She didn't look up until he was almost on top
of her.

"Oh, Captain," she said. "I didn't hear you come in."
She began to laugh softly to herself—everyone was laughing except him, Moses thought, he'd missed the joke—but
it didn't last.

"What happened to him?"

"I did. Where's Deacon, Moses?"

"Deacon's dead."

Something broke behind those glistening eyes. She lowered her head to her knees, and her small frame shook with the suppressed sobs. After a time she raised her head again, ignoring the tears that flowed unobstructed down her cheeks.

"They had him all walled up in there, Moses, all boxed in with all the garbage they gave him. I couldn't make him do what I wanted—that would have made me like them . . . like him." She nodded at the corpse. "So I just pulled down all their walls, and told him he could do what he wanted. And look at the difference it made."

Then she could restrain the sobbing no longer.

"We should get out of here," Moses said, at length.

She looked up at him. "It wasn't me, Moses. Just the one time, and that was an accident. It was."

"You scared the hell out of me, girl."

"I know. I'm sorry."

"I don't know what you are anymore, Spooky. I don't know how to live with something like that."

"I'm who I always was, Moses."

"I know. That's what I can't stop thinking about."

"Yeah . . ."

The one duffel bag did little to fill the open passenger lock.

Mitsuko dropped its heavy companion beside it, and then turned back into the ship for the last time. She was vaguely aware of Moses off somewhere within the bowels of the *Goose*, but she scrupulously forced herself not to probe for him. It would have served no purpose.

She looked around the engine room, the comforting metal box that had hidden her for so long, borne her away from the pain of human contact. She would miss its protection, worse than she could possibly express. But it was gone. Finished. She locked shut the small toolbox, her own personal gear, and headed back for the lock.

He was standing there, one bag over his shoulder, the other in his right hand. He scowled at her fiercely.

"If I thought for one second you were making me do this, I'd throw you out right on your little Japanese ass, you hear me?"

But she couldn't answer him, her face tight against the

fabric of his coverall, her arms scarcely meeting around his barrel chest. Finally, when she could trust herself to speak, she looked up at him, grinning like an idiot.

"You're not scared?"

"Don't be stupid. Of course I am. But when wasn't I ever?"

*The towering new science fiction epic by the author of*
*RISSA KERGUELEN and THE DEMU TRILOGY*

# STAR REBEL
# by F.M. Busby

At thirteen, Bran Tregare was stripped of his home, his name and his family, and sent to the brutal space academy known as the Slaughterhouse. At twenty, he'd survived the sadistic discipline of a starcaptain called the Butcher to become an ace pilot, crack gunner and hardened killer. At twenty-one, he escaped with an armed warship to begin a one-man war against Earth's imperial masters.

STAR REBEL is a searing portrait of a man whose vengeance was forged in the dark heart of empire.

Read STAR REBEL, on sale January 15, 1984 wherever Bantam paperbacks are sold or use the handy coupon below for ordering:

# OUT OF THIS WORLD!

That's the only way to describe Bantam's great series of science fiction classics. These space-age thrillers are filled with terror, fancy and adventure and written by America's most renowned writers of science fiction. Welcome to outer space and have a good trip!

# FANTASY AND SCIENCE FICTION FAVORITES

Bantam brings you the recognized classics as well as the current favorites in fantasy and science fiction. Here you will find the most recent titles by the most respected authors in the genre.

| | | | |
|---|---|---|---|
| ☐ | 23944 | THE DEEP  John Crowley | $2.95 |
| ☐ | 23853 | THE SHATTERED STARS  Richard McEnroe | $2.95 |
| ☐ | 23795 | DAMIANO  R. A. MacAvoy | $2.95 |
| ☐ | 23205 | TEA WITH THE BLACK DRAGON  R. A. MacAvoy | $2.75 |
| ☐ | 23365 | THE SHUTTLE PEOPLE  George Bishop | $2.95 |
| ☐ | 22939 | THE UNICORN CREED  Elizabeth Scarborough | $3.50 |
| ☐ | 23120 | THE MACHINERIES OF JOY  Ray Bradbury | $2.75 |
| ☐ | 22666 | THE GREY MANE OF MORNING  Joy Chant | $3.50 |
| ☐ | 23494 | MASKS OF TIME  Robert Silverberg | $2.95 |
| ☐ | 23057 | THE BOOK OF SKULLS  Robert Silverberg | $2.95 |
| ☐ | 23063 | LORD VALENTINE'S CASTLE  Robert Silverberg | $3.50 |
| ☐ | 20870 | JEM  Frederik Pohl | $2.95 |
| ☐ | 23460 | DRAGONSONG  Anne McCaffrey | $2.95 |
| ☐ | 20592 | TIME STORM  Gordon R. Dickson | $2.95 |
| ☐ | 23036 | BEASTS  John Crowley | $2.95 |
| ☐ | 23666 | EARTHCHILD  Sharon Webb | $2.95 |

**Prices and availability subject to change without notice.**

**Buy them at your local bookstore or use this handy coupon for ordering:**

---

Bantam Books, Inc., Dept. SF2, 414 East Golf Road, Des Plaines, Ill. 60016

Please send me the books I have checked above. I am enclosing $_____
(please add $1.25 to cover postage and handling). Send check or money order
—no cash or C.O.D.'s please.

Mr/Mrs/Miss _____

Address_____

City_____ State/Zip_____

SF2—1/84

Please allow four to six weeks for delivery. This offer expires 7/84.